FAT CAT TAKES THE CAKE

Janet Cantrell

BERKLEY PRIME CRIME, NEW YORK

An imprint of Penguin Random House LLC
375 Hudson Street, New York, New York 10014

FAT CAT TAKES THE CAKE

A Berkley Prime Crime Book / published by arrangement with the author

ISBN: 978-0-425-26744-8

PUBLISHING HISTORY
Berkley Prime Crime mass-market edition / April 2016

PRINTED IN THE UNITED STATES OF AMERICA

10 9 8 7 6 5 4 3 2 1

Cover illustration by Craig White.
Cover design by George Long.
Interior text design by Kelly Lipovich.

Penguin
Random
House

To my husband, Cliff

ACKNOWLEDGMENTS

I would like to acknowledge a few of the people who have helped me with this book. For information on hacking, Cori Lynn Arnold and James M. Jackson. For details on evasive maneuvers, Sam Morton. For giving me spot-on feedback, Gale Albright and Paula Benson. My Plothatcher friends, as always, Janet Bolin, Janet Koch/Laurie Cass, Pam Cochran, Krista Davis, Daryl Wood Gerber, and Marilyn Levinson, for much needed and invaluable moral support.

ONE

"That's a lot of mail," Anna Larson said. She was taking a short afternoon break, sitting on the squeaky stool at the work island in the kitchen of the Bar None, the dessert bar shop co-owned by her and Charity Oliver, called Chase by almost everyone.

"Look!" Chase waved an envelope at Anna. Her eyes were bright and her cheeks red, partly from coming inside out of the early December cold, but also from excitement.

"If you held it still, I could see it."

Chase smiled at her business partner and surrogate grandmother. "I'll do better than that. I'll open it for you."

"You know that's a federal offense," Julie Larson said.

"Julie." Anna put on her stern-grandparent face, which

1

looked incongruous with her soft gray hair and her periwinkle eyes, much more used to smiling. "You don't always have to be a lawyer." Anna wore her usual bright sweater with a plain T-shirt and jeans. This sweater was a rough, burlap-like material in aqua and bright green, worn over a pale blue shirt.

"But it *is*, Grandma." Julie, sitting next to Anna, nudged the older woman slightly and fished a marshmallow out of her cocoa with a spoon. Her eyes were identical to Anna's, but set into a face that was forty years younger than Anna's seventy-two and framed by dark brown hair. She kept her hair short and practical for her new job with Bud Ellison's small real estate firm. Chase thought her good friend seemed much happier and more relaxed since she had left the district attorney's office.

"Your honor," Anna began.

"That's for judges, Grandma," Julie said.

"Your high horse-ness, then. I give Charity permission to open my mail. Wait." She took the envelope Chase was still waving in front of her. "Who is it from?" Anna saw the return address. "It's the Batter Battle!" She ripped the envelope open and pulled several sheets of paper from it, quickly scanning the cover letter. "I've been invited to participate in the Minny Batter Battle."

After fanning her face in amazement, she slipped off the stool, leaving the seat spinning and creaking, and danced around the kitchen.

Chase watched her with amusement. "This is a big deal, I take it?"

"Anyone can apply to enter the Battle," Julie explained.

"But only a few are selected for invitations every year. Grandma hasn't gotten an invitation before."

"This'll show that Grace Pilsen," Anna said. "She's called me three years in a row to tell me she was invited. And to gloat. That Grace Pilsen." Anna gritted her teeth at the thought.

Anna's cell phone rang. She looked at the ID and grunted.

"Who is it?" Julie asked.

"That Grace Pilsen, I'll bet," Chase mouthed. The woman owned a bakery called The Pilsener. Anna was quite vocal about her opinion that using the word *the* in the shop name was pretentious. Chase thought The Pilsener sounded very much like a beer shop, but no alcohol at all was available there.

"Hello? Grace?"

Chase and Julie high-fived behind Anna's back.

"You did? That's nice," Anna said, grimacing. "Yes, I know. Yes, I know. Yes, you've told me that. I think we must get our mail at the exact same time. I got mine just now, too . . . What do you think? The same thing you got. Listen, I'm very busy. I'll call you later."

Anna turned to the two young women with a smile that crinkled the corners of her eyes. "That felt good."

"So, *that Grace Pilsen* got hers today, too?" Julie asked. "I was hoping she wouldn't get invited this year."

"That's a little too much to hope for," Anna said. "She helped found the Minny Batter Battle, after all. I believe the name was her idea. After all, she thought up the awful name of The Pilsener for her own place."

"Minny for Minneapolis, I guess. How long has it been going on?" Chase asked. She had moved back to Minneapolis from Chicago last year and didn't remember the contest from before she left.

"Three years," Julie said. "But, Grandma, just because she was on the original committee doesn't mean she should take up one of the invitational slots every year."

"I agree." Anna shuffled through the application papers that had also been in the envelope. "She doesn't even have a hand in the organizing anymore. But it is what it is."

Anna had a great philosophy, Chase thought. "True." She started humming "I Dreamed a Dream" from *Les Miserables* and headed for the small office that housed the computer Chase used to pay bills. It was off the kitchen, near the rear door.

She stuck a leg through the door before entering to keep Quincy from escaping.

The butterscotch tabby jumped down from the computer keyboard where he'd been napping, alert at the sound of the doorknob turning. It was early for evening din dins. He peered up at the friendly human, the one who fed him his meals and treats. The way his ears pricked and his eyes brightened, you would think he expected a treat. That was not to be. She merely threw a stack of mail onto the desk, next to the keyboard that was still warm from the cat's body, stooped to rub his head, setting off his rumbling purr, and left.

The cat was left to swish his tail in annoyance, then resume his nap.

❖

Inger Uhlgren, one of the salesclerks, was entering the kitchen for her break when Chase returned.

"I'll check back later," Julie said. "I have to go buy some groceries for myself." She waved and went out to the large parking lot behind the building.

"It's wild today," Inger said, hopping onto the stool Anna had vacated. "Maybe I shouldn't take my break." She took another look at Anna's beaming face. "What's up, Mrs. Larson?"

Anna told her about getting invited to the Batter Battle.

"Congratulations!" Inger jumped off the stool to give her employer a hug.

"Look at you, leaping around," Anna said, holding Inger at arm's length to inspect her tiny baby bump. "You must be feeling a lot better."

"I am, finally. The morning sickness went away a few days ago." It was so good to see a smile on her pretty face. Inger's delicate coloring—gray eyes, blonde curls over a wide forehead—combined with her small stature, made her seem like a fragile doll. She made both Chase and Anna want to take care of her.

"I'll go," Chase said. "You go ahead and take your break. You probably need to drink something."

"Yes, ma'am, Ms. Oliver." Inger gave Chase a mock salute.

"Call me Chase." *Why did her employees all insist on*

calling her Ms. Oliver? She grabbed a salesroom smock off the hook by the swinging double doors that led to the front of the shop, thinking how relieved she was that Inger's morning sickness was gone. The poor girl had gotten pregnant shortly before her fiancé got shipped overseas with the military and killed in battle. On top of that, her parents had thrown her out when she told them she was expecting. Chase, Anna, and Julie had all stepped in to make sure she had a place to stay, trading her off among themselves, until her parents relented and took her back in, briefly. Inger had made all the arrangements and was due to move into her own apartment soon, a short walk from the shop. Chase still felt that they should all watch over her, not trusting the uneasy truce in the Uhlgren family.

Chase entered her salesroom with a huge smile. She couldn't help it; she was so proud of the Bar None. She and Anna were co-owners, but Chase had designed the salesroom on her own. She took a moment to enjoy the wallpaper with broad stripes of raspberry and vanilla, the cotton-candy-pink shelves ranked along the sidewalls, the small round tables heaped with boxes of treats, and the glass display case at the rear.

This month, garlands of fake pine, tied with pink bows, looped above the shelves. Chase and Anna had opted for a pink-and-green Christmas décor, noting that red and green would look fairly awful with all the pink in the shop. Anna had placed a few white poinsettias in the corners and Inger had taken it upon herself to string up the holiday cards the Bar None had received. They hung on a long green ribbon behind the shiny glass case.

She took another glance at the glass. Oops, not so shiny at the moment. Smudges, from fingers pointing to selections on the shelves, were inevitable. It would have to wait for a cleaning, though. The shop was too busy now.

A family with five small children was leaving. No doubt those wee fingers were responsible for the latest smears near the bottom of the case. Even with the family of seven gone, the room was crowded.

The newest employee, Mallory Tucker, was behind the counter ringing up sales, so Chase circulated among the browsers, explaining the contents of the boxes, from telling a middle-aged couple that Harvest Bars did indeed contain pumpkin and related spices, to pointing out to a pair of teenage girls that they could order a box of six with mixed dessert bars. They had been arguing because one of them wanted Peanut Butter Fudge Bars (she didn't like coconut), the other wanted Hula Bars (she didn't care for chocolate).

As soon as Inger returned from her break, of course, the customers thinned out. Chase returned to the kitchen with Mallory, so their newest hire could take her break.

Anna sat at the island again, perusing the application to the Minny Batter Battle, her purse on the counter. She must have gotten it out of the office, Chase thought.

"Oh, your phone dinged," Anna said, still staring at the papers.

Chase's phone was on the granite counter next to the refrigerator. She would get it next time she got up. Her feet were tired. Chase sat between Mallory and Anna.

"How are you holding up?" Anna asked Mallory. She had been working at the Bar None for only a week.

"Is it always this busy?" The young woman looked exhausted. Her long blonde hair was shiny, as were her eyes, but her shoulders drooped. Mallory had graduated from high school in the spring. In spite of that, in addition to babysitting, she had listed a long string of part-time and temporary jobs on her application. This was her first real payroll job, though. Anna and Chase had both been impressed by her earnestness and sincerity during her interview. So many of the applicants treated the whole experience as something frivolous, some even checking their phones repeatedly while Anna or Chase tried to get them to answer questions about themselves. So far, they both thought they had made the right choice. Mallory seldom smiled, but got along well with Inger, which was important. Her new employee was probably still a bit nervous on the job, Chase thought.

"It's not always *this* busy," Chase said. "This time between Thanksgiving and the holidays is one of the two busiest of the year."

"In January," Anna said, "we'll probably only need one of you at a time, so you won't need to come in all day, every day." Anna got up to get Mallory something to drink. "Pop? Coffee? There might be some more lemonade."

"Lemonade, please." She gulped it down. She had obviously been thirsty. "I'll go back to the front now."

"Stay another few minutes if you like," Chase said. She didn't want to wear out their new employee right away.

"That bell keeps ringing."

It was true. Since Chase had left the front room, the bell on the front door had tinkled every three seconds. The shop might be full again by now. Mallory climbed off the stool and scooted into the salesroom.

"Baking all done?" Chase asked Anna.

"Everything except washing up." Anna glanced at her watch.

"I'll do that, Anna. I'll bet you have things to do, don't you?"

"Everything should be ready for the wedding. If not, it's too late."

"I can't believe it. It's in three weeks! I know our dresses are ordered, but Julie and I still need shoes," Chase said.

"Three weeks exactly. You know I offered to make the dresses."

Yes, Anna had. And she would have and they would have been beautiful, but Chase and Julie wanted to spare her, the bride, that extra chore. If they all ended up worrying about the arrival of the bridesmaid dresses, though, it would have been better for Anna to make them.

"I would like to leave early, though," Anna said, "to take this home and fill it out." She stuffed the application papers into her purse.

"When is the Batter Battle?"

"Two and a half weeks from now. But the deadline to sign up is this coming Saturday. I have to turn in a recipe, so I have to come up with one by then."

"Can't you use one of our best sellers from here?"

Anna shrugged into her parka. "I'd rather create some-thing. I have no idea what."

Chase sought inspiration in the ceiling for a moment. "You

9

were working on the ones that tasted like donuts, remember? A couple of months ago? Did you quit working on them?"

Anna paused on her way to the door. "Yes, I did. Those weren't going to work. Much too heavy. But I've been fiddling around with muffin recipes. Muffin Cookie Bars, I think I would call them. That would be different, wouldn't it?"

"Would you rather call them muffins or cookies? Muffins would be more unusual. But are they sweet enough? Muffins often have a topping."

"You may be right, Charity. I'll try a topping at home tonight. Game on, Grace Pilsen."

"Bring them in tomorrow," Chase shouted as Anna left.

She was now alone in the kitchen with dirty bowls and baking pans, but also with the sweet aroma of Cherry Chiffon Bars, the last thing Anna had baked.

At six, closing time, Chase turned the sign on the front door over to "Closed." After Inger and Mallory left, it was Quincy's time.

This time, when the office door opened, no one hindered the eager cat. He knew the nightly routine. In spite of some extra heft around his middle, which some people thought made him look even cuter, he easily leapt to the countertop next to the stove. From experience, he kept away from the burners, even though they were cool now. He was intent on finding crumbs. When dessert bars were transferred from baking pans to display bins, there were invariably crumbs.

Chase watched Quincy, patrolling and purring, with affection. He'd been such a scrawny, frightened little kitten when she first saw him, newly rescued from the beach, where his litter had been abandoned. She had hesitated only a moment, picking out one of the six. Quincy's large amber eyes spoke to her and, when she picked him up, he snuggled his way into her heart.

She heard her phone dinging. It was still next to the refrigerator. When Quincy finished with the counters, she would disinfect them, but first, she'd better find out who was texting her. She remembered that she had gotten a text earlier and had ignored it.

It was from Julie and read, "Open your mail and call me."

The mail was in the office where she'd dropped it. Most of it, the part that wasn't junk mail and more greeting cards, was probably bills, so putting them next to the computer where she paid them was a good place. A wastebasket sat next to the desk for most of the mail.

One piece, though, was not junk, not even a bill. How had she not noticed it when she'd picked out the envelope from the Minny Batter Battle? This one was from Hammond, her high school. She ripped it open as she called Julie.

"A reunion?" she said when Julie answered. "Did you get an invitation, too?"

"Yes, and look at the date," Julie said. "It's this coming Saturday!"

"Three days from now? That's awfully quick."

"And who has a reunion in December?"

Chase noticed the name on the bottom of the paper. "Guess who? Dickie Byrd."

"That figures. What do you wanna bet he's running for some office somewhere?"

"I won't bet against that," Chase said. Richard Byrd, always called Dickie behind his back—and sometimes to his face—had been their class president. Not because of his leadership qualities, but because of Monique's ability to mount an unbeatable campaign. Richard and Monique had married while still in college and Richard was now on the school board. No one who knew both of them doubted that his sights were aimed higher. "Still, if he has a reunion to announce he's running for office, that's pretty tacky."

"I'm going," Julie said. "There are a lot of people I'd like to see again. So many of our classmates moved out of state."

"Me included, but I came back."

"What are you wearing?" When Chase didn't answer, Julie insisted they go shopping that night. "The stores are still open."

Chase knew she was in good hands with Julie, a champion shopper. They whizzed through three stores and both went home satisfied.

As Chase readied herself for bed in her apartment above the shop, she went over some of the people she'd gone to high school with. There were some she wouldn't mind seeing again. But she sure didn't want to run into Eddie Heath.

TWO

The day after Chase and Julie had gotten their reunion notices, Julie came by for an early morning bike ride. The two best friends enjoyed their bike rides together and didn't get to do them as often as they would like lately. Julie was settling into her new job and, from what Chase could tell, being in real estate law would mean less stress and fewer hours than working in the DA's office.

White twinkle lights were strung in the thin branches of the trees that grew along the sidewalks. They weren't lit now, but the area was a fairyland at night in December. They pedaled down Fourteenth Avenue SE, over to University Avenue, and onto the Tenth Street bridge. When they reached the middle, they stopped to watch the river. Chase always felt something switch on inside her soul, something that glowed with a serene light, when she stood and gazed at the peaceful Mississippi as it flowed beneath her.

"So, what do you think?" Julie asked after a moment.

"About?"

"Is Dickie Byrd running for office?"

"Why else would he call an impromptu class reunion?" Chase said. "It's fourteen years since we graduated. He couldn't wait for fifteen?"

"Still, we have to go."

"Well, yah. We bought new outfits." Chase had gotten out her outfit again in the morning and re-examined it. She still liked it. They both bought jacket dresses. Julie's had a short, flouncy, flirty skirt that matched her favorite silk scarf, while Chase's was a bit longer with a draped-front jacket. The sale rack at Macy's had been a gold mine. When you went shopping with Julie, you got results. That woman was a shopper.

"Didn't he run for mayor of Minneapolis recently?" Julie asked.

A pair of mallards floated past, in the middle of the river, avoiding the ice beginning to form at the shoreline. Chase wondered what they were still doing in Minnesota. Maybe they hung out at a hot spring somewhere for the winter.

"Three years ago," Chase said. "He lost by a lot, as I recall. I'll bet ten dollars he's going to run again next time."

"I won't bet against that, but I'll bet you twenty he loses again." Julie grinned.

Chase's cell phone trilled. Julie raised her eyebrows and Chase shrugged to show she didn't know who was calling. "Yes?"

"This is Ron North, Chase. Remember me?" The voice

was unfamiliar. A man's voice, but not very deep. An image of a skinny, sweaty guy was forming.

She frowned. His face was back there in the nether part of her brain, but out of reach. "I'm sorry—"

"Reporter for the *Herald Gopher*."

"Okay." She subscribed to that paper, but couldn't remember seeing his name in it.

"Hey, we went to Hammond High together. I worked for the school paper then."

Chase had worked for the school paper, but didn't recall that Ron North had. At first. She dug a little further into her memories. Now she had him. A small, thin, wiry, nervous guy.

"Oh. Yes?" Why was he calling her?

"I was wondering. I got a idea for a article." *An* idea for *an* article, she corrected him mentally. "I'd like to do a piece called 'Local Girl Makes Good.' You got that shop, right? That bakery?"

"I co-own the Bar None. It's a dessert bar shop. That's the only thing we bake."

"Hey, don't sell yourself short. Those're good. So, what do you say?"

"To what?" She frowned and shook her head at Julie, who probably thought Chase was fending off a cable salesman.

"I'll come by, do an interview, snap some shots. Get you in the paper."

"When?"

"I'll let you know. Talk to you later."

With that, he was gone. "That was odd." She told Julie about the call.

"I remember him well. Don't you?" Julie made a sour face.

15

Her hands, shaking her handlebars, sent tremors through her bike. "He had the most annoying crush on me. I couldn't get rid of him for the longest time."

"Oh, was he the stalker guy? How could I forget?"

"I'll never forget." Julie glanced at her watch. "Gotta get back." She turned her bike and jumped onto the seat.

"Me, too."

Chase remembered Ron clearly now. Julie had been greatly disturbed by the persistent, annoying, unwanted attention. She had started staying in at night, not socializing. Then, suddenly, he had switched his obsession to someone else and Julie had started living again.

An hour later Chase was showered and opening up the Bar None. The shop was busy in December and got busier the closer they came to the holidays. It was three weeks until Christmas. The tinkling bell on the front door got a workout all morning.

The two salesclerks worked in the front, Anna baked in the kitchen, and Chase worked in the office on orders and payments. When Chase finished up her computer work mid-morning, she went out front to help.

"Chase, how are you?"

It was that reedy, young-sounding, male voice. She was surprised to see Ron North in the shop.

"Did we set a time?" She was sure they hadn't.

"I had an errand across the street and saw, hey, here was your store." He dug a notebook and pencil out of his jacket pocket and propped his skinny hip on one of the small display tables, dislodging a stack of dessert bar boxes.

Chase jumped to catch them before they hit the floor.

"Oh, sorry." He fiddled with the pencil between two fingers, then dug a few peanuts out of his pocket and tossed them into his mouth.

She was recalling more bits and pieces about him. She remembered how he had always made her nervous when he was hanging around Julie. He was full of tics and usually sweaty. She remembered now that he had been on the school newspaper staff until he had to leave because of his grades. The smell of peanuts emanating from him triggered her memory, too. He had always reeked of peanuts.

As she restacked the boxes he continued. "How about that article? 'Local Girl Makes Good'? Looks like you have a nice place here. You own it, right?"

"I'm the co-owner," Chase answered cautiously. "Anna Larson owns the Bar None with me." She wasn't sure she wanted Ron North to do an article on her. She glanced around at the full shop. "This isn't a good time to chat, Ron. Maybe another time?"

"Sure, sure. I'll just walk around and get some local flavor. Get it? Flavor?"

Chase gave him a wan smile and nodded, then moved on to people who were interested in buying dessert bars.

A young couple stood frowning at the display case while Mallory was busy taking money from two college coeds for two boxes of Margarita Cheesecake Bars. Chase explained what some of the ingredients were in several types of bars, keeping track of Ron North out of the corner of her eye. She hoped he wouldn't knock any more boxes down.

He strolled beside the pink shelves on the sidewall filled with boxes and bumped another table, but not hard enough to topple the stack of boxes. She couldn't figure out what he was doing. He wasn't, she was sure, interested in buying, and she had told him she couldn't talk. Maybe he was waiting for a lull in business? Good luck, she thought. It might stay like this until six.

Chase's next surprise was seeing Dickie and Monique Byrd walk into the store.

"Charity Oliver," Dickie boomed, sticking out his hand.

At the moment, she wasn't waiting on any customers. She shook his outstretched hand, soft and dry, wondering if he had looked her up in the yearbook immediately before dropping in. If he remembered her, he'd call her Chase. No one called her Charity except Anna.

"Maybe we don't need to have a reunion if everyone is going to come into my shop," Chase said, using a smile and a tilt of her head to soften her words. "Ron North is here, too."

"Ho, ho, ho!" Dickie sounded like Santa Claus.

"Monique, nice to see you again." Chase reached to shake his wife's hand since he wasn't going to acknowledge that she was there. The woman kept her hands to herself and stared at Chase's. That's a little odd, Chase thought. Chase peeked at her own hand in case it was covered in dough or powdered sugar. That wouldn't have surprised her, but it seemed clean.

Ron was inching toward the front door.

"I wondered if you could do me a big favor," Dickie said. "Mona, give Charity a poster."

Chase remembered that Monique had been called Mona in school. Sometimes she was called Mona the Mouth because she talked so much. Chattered on and on about nothing. It seemed she had gotten over that. Or maybe she couldn't get a word in with Dickie running off at the mouth like he did.

Monique caught sight of Ron North and flinched, her eyes wide and frightened for a split second. Ron seemed to sneer at her, then threw open the door and left. Monique returned her attention to them, completely composed. She dipped into the large, heavy-looking bag she carried and pulled out a roll of paper. She unfurled what proved to be an eleven-by-seventeen-inch poster, which she handed to Chase, being careful not to touch hands or fingers.

Her phobia about touching people suddenly clicked in Chase's memory. Monique was a little unusual.

A startlingly large picture of Dickie's oversized head, in full grin, stared out at her. If Julie had bet with her about him running for mayor again, she would have won. It was a campaign poster touting "Rich Byrd for Mayor."

Good luck, she thought, changing your nickname to Rich.

Monique had seen her draw back to read the large print. "Isn't it lovely?" she said, showing all of her huge, white teeth. With those and her perfectly coifed helmet, her stylish belted suit and high-heeled mid-length boots, she was ready to step into the role of mayor's wife and pose for photographs. Maybe even for a portrait above the mantel.

"Did you do it?" She remembered that Monique ran

Dickie's campaign for class president, which had been much more successful than his first run for mayor. Chase thought he was still on the young side to be a mayor—most of the members of their class were about thirty-two years old—but some towns had young mayors.

"I did." Monique beamed even brighter. "Here, it's yours."

Chase tried to hand it to her. "That's okay. I don't need one." Monique stepped back and kept her hands at her side.

"Charity," Dickie said, moving in close. "We'd love your support. If you could just put this in the corner of your window, we'd appreciate it so much."

Chase thought as quickly as she could. She couldn't endorse this guy. "I'll have to ask my business partner."

"We'll wait. We can shop for some desserts, can't we, Mona?"

No way was she going to put up his poster. "She isn't here right now." She threw a stern frown at Mallory, who was nearby, eavesdropping, so she wouldn't give Chase away. "I'll consult her later."

Chase took the poster and retreated to the kitchen.

THREE

A t the end of the day, Chase flipped the sign and everyone trooped into the kitchen to help clean up.

Chase loved this time of day. Everyone could relax and she could revel in the fact that this cute, sweet-smelling place was part hers. She never got tired of doing that. She opened the office door and let Quincy out to prowl.

Anna answered a knock on the back door and let in Dr. Michael Ramos. He was Quincy's veterinarian and Chase had begun dating him a short time ago. At least she thought they were dating. The actual dates were few and far between since they were both so busy. They talked on the phone a lot more often than they saw each other.

Quincy ran over to rub some orange hair onto Dr. Ramos's slacks.

"You quit that," Chase mock scolded. "Look what you've done."

Mike chuckled, a deep, rumbly sound that thrilled Chase's insides. He picked Quincy up and rubbed the stripes between his ears. After he set Quincy down, Mike settled on a stool.

"Can I get you something to drink?" Anna asked.

"No, you're all busy. I only wanted to touch base." He looked directly at Chase with those liquid brown eyes. "I haven't seen you for over a week."

It had been longer than that, she thought. "How would you like to go with me to my high school reunion?" she asked.

"What year is it?"

"Fourteen."

He shook his head, puzzled.

"It's not a reunion year. Our class president is running for mayor and I think it's more of a campaign rally. But he's calling it a reunion and using the high school gym for it." She sat down next to him to convince him to accompany her.

Mike didn't reply.

"You'd get to meet all my classmates."

"Like who?"

"Julie graduated with me."

"Yes, I know that."

"I don't keep in touch with many of them, but it'll be fun to catch up with them again." Except for Eddie Heath. But if Mike were there, Eddie's presence wouldn't bother her so much.

"Here you go, little fella," Mallory said, sprinkling the remains of a Peanut Butter Fudge bar she had been nibbling in front of Quincy.

Chase jumped off her stool. "No!" she shouted, ran to the counter, and swept up the dessert bar bits.

Mallory took a step back, amazement and a bit of fear on her face.

"Sorry to startle you," Chase said. "But cats can't have chocolate. It's very bad for them."

"Really? My dad used to give our cat, Mittens, the last bite of his chocolate bar all the time."

"A little won't hurt them," Mike said. "But it's a good policy not to give it to cats. Besides, Quincy doesn't need anything extra."

Chase finally managed to extract a promise from Mike that he would accompany her to the reunion on Saturday. It might be a fun night, she thought.

After Mike kissed her good-bye and Inger left, Anna said, "It's time. I have to turn in my recipe Saturday for the Batter Battle."

Mallory had stayed to finish putting away the baking utensils. "Already?" she said.

"What do you have?" Chase asked.

"The basic muffin dough part is good, I think. But it feels like I need something else. I've tried putting a cinnamon-sugar crumb topping on them, but didn't like the way that turned out. It's so messy."

"What else have you tried?" Mallory asked, closing the drawer on the last of the whisks.

"I tried to do a thick vanilla frosting. That made them too sticky-sweet."

"What about adding blueberries? That's my favorite muffin."

"Blueberries. Yes, that's what's missing. And what goes on top?"

"How about a vanilla drizzle?"

Anna considered for a moment. "We don't have any with drizzled icing. Mostly powdered-sugar toppings. That might work. It would be different."

"And you could put some sherry flavoring in them," Mallory said with excitement. "I saw a bottle of that in the grocery store last week and I've been trying to think where a person would use it. I think it would be pretty good."

"Sherry flavoring? Excellent," Anna said. "Let's do it."

The three of them stayed late working on the recipe. Near midnight, they all left the kitchen, happy with the results. Anna's Blueberry Muffin Bar recipe might be a winner at the Minny Batter Battle.

Chase felt like three was a crowd as she walked into the Hammond High School gymnasium with Julie and Jay Wright, the tall, dimpled criminal defense attorney Julie was dating. Chase gritted her teeth at the thought that Mike Ramos had stood her up at the last minute. She'd told him about the reunion Thursday night. Then, the very next day, he remembered an out-of-town conference for the AVMA in Albuquerque. Some old veterinarians' group. He flew out Friday and was getting home late Saturday. She hoped he had to buy a last-minute plane ticket that cost a fortune. That would serve him right for preferring a bunch of stupid animal doctors to her company.

She and Julie had ridden over together through the cold

rain in Chase's Ford Fusion. The reunion was slated to start at eight o'clock and end at midnight. They'd timed their arrival to be fashionably late, at eight thirty. On the way, Julie said she had a problem and she needed Chase's input.

"Sure. Shoot."

"You remember Professor Fear? The guy who lives next door to Hilda Bjorn?"

Chase nodded, concentrating on the dark, slick streets.

Hilda Bjorn had nearly been killed because she knew too much when Gabe Naughtly, who lived across the street from the elderly woman, was murdered. In the course of things, she became a fan of the Bar None. Her neighbor, a university professor, looked after the old woman. Ms. Bjorn also seemed to look after him, since he was quite absent-minded.

"Andy Fear called our office and asked for some advice. Since I'm the new gal, they gave him to me. Translation: This is a low-paying job."

"I wouldn't think he would have a lot of extra money for lawyers."

"He doesn't. I got permission to make this a pro bono case, especially after I delved into it."

"Now you have me curious." She braked for a red light. Red-and-green blinking lights from a nearby shop window blended in the wet reflection of the stoplight and taillights ahead of her. The wipers were only on medium speed, but she was considering turning them to high. The pattering rain-drops were becoming more insistent.

"He wants me to go over an offer that Ms. Bjorn got for her house."

"She's selling her house?" Chase was surprised at that. The light changed and she started up.

"No, she's not. That's what he found odd. She got the offer out of the blue from someone who came to her door."

Chase frowned as she turned the wipers to high. "You brought an umbrella, I hope," she said to Julie. "What did you find out?"

"Nothing yet. I'm going over to talk to her tomorrow. I'm sure I'll tell her not to take the offer. Professor Fear said the amount was ridiculously low. It sounded high to Ms. Bjorn because she bought her house so long ago and the offer is much more than she paid."

After their dash through the rain, they arrived at the gym laughing. Jay Wright was waiting at the door for Julie. Chase made a beeline for the punch bowl. She would have to have a drink early so it would be out of her system by the time she had to drive home through the deluge.

Bart Fender stood at the punch bowl like he was guarding it and the delicious-looking cake beside the other goodies.

"Is it any good?" she asked the former star wrestler for Hammond High. She remembered he was a strong-looking guy back then, but his muscles were almost terrifying now.

His smile came across as strained. Maybe because of the acne damage to his face. "It's all right. I've got a little something extra if you'd like to add it."

"No thanks. This will be fine." She dipped herself a punch cup of the red liquid and sipped. Sweet and gooey, with a tiny hint of rum. She wished she had been on the punch committee for this gala. Then they would have had

26

decent punch. At least she wouldn't have to worry about driving after drinking this.

"Do you think our boy has a chance this time?" she asked Bart, staring up at the "Vote for Rich Byrd" banners strung from the ceiling.

He turned his head and raised his eyes to them, displaying a shiny dome. "You got me." He had had nice hair when he was younger, she remembered. Bart Fender had been a local hero, winning the state wrestling championship for Hammond both his junior and senior years.

"There you are." Julie and Jay came to the table for some punch.

"How is it?" Jay asked.

Chase stuck her tongue out and pointed her finger to it, the universal symbol for "so awful it gags me."

"Oh well," Julie said. "It's wet."

A trio of men approached Jay. "We need an impartial judge to settle a bet. How much do you know about football?"

Julie groaned. "He knows just about everything."

"Come over here, then. It won't take but a minute."

"Be right back," Jay said, and left with them.

Bart had left, too, so Chase was alone for a moment with Julie.

They both noticed that Dickie Byrd's voice was rising above the moderate din.

"I'd say the guest of honor is enjoying his party," Julie said.

"Getting a little tipsy," Chase agreed. "He sure isn't getting looped on this insipid, sweet punch. It tastes like that fake strawberry flavoring that Anna tried out once. Awful stuff."

"Look at Monique. I would say she's not pleased, wouldn't you?"

Chase saw her, a few feet away from the circle around her husband. She yanked at her hair, which prompted Chase to remember how she used to pull it out when she was stressed in high school.

"Oops. I'd say the campaign manager is upset."

"Oh no," Julie said softly. "Save me."

"Julie, where have you been? I've been waiting and waiting for you to show up." It was Ron North, who, Chase thought, must have been adding his own juice to the punch, too. He lurched toward them, leering at Julie and breathing out the mixed aromas of peanuts and whiskey.

Chase felt the hairs on the nape of her neck rise.

"I heard you were part'a that real estate scam. True?"

"What are you talking about?" Julie inched away from Ron. Chase heard her breath quicken.

He stepped closer, invading her personal space. "The lowball offers. I know you're involved."

Julie gave an exasperated puff, backed up some more, and sipped her punch.

"You don' wanna drink any a tha' stuff. Here, I got good stuff." He dug a small flask from his pocket and attempted to pour some into Julie's cup.

Chase would have to remember to carry a flask at the next class reunion. Everyone seemed to know to do that but her.

Julie snatched her punch away before the stream could hit her cup and the strong-smelling bourbon poured onto the floor.

"Now look wha' you did." Ron gave Julie an ugly sneer. "You're gonna have to make that up to me."

Before either Chase or Julie could react, he grabbed Julie's short brown hair, pulled her forward, and mashed her face into his.

Julie shoved him away, but he grabbed on to her silk scarf.

By that time Jay had seen what was going on and had returned.

"That's enough, buddy," he said to Ron, tapping his shoulder. "You need to leave this lady alone."

Since Jay towered over him, Ron staggered backward, bumping the sturdy punch table. He managed to stay upright as he stuffed Julie's scarf into his hip pocket, and put up his hands to fend Jay off.

Julie and Jay hurried away and Chase decided not to stick around Ron North any longer either. While everyone stared at the commotion, Chase crept away and left Ron by himself at the punch bowl.

Chase found some women who had been in her senior Honors English class and joined in their conversation about what they'd been doing since high school. Two were married with small children at home and three were working locally. They all showed interest in visiting the Bar None when Chase told them about it.

"Did you hear about Dillon Yardley?" one of the moms asked.

Two of them nodded but Chase said she hadn't heard.

"Is she still in a coma?"

"A coma?" Chase asked. "What happened?"

"She tried to kill herself," the first mom whispered.

"No wonder Bart isn't having a good time," said the other mom.

"Why is that?" Chase said.

"They were going together."

Chase shuddered. Poor Bart Fender. He did seem pretty grim, but she couldn't blame him if his girlfriend was in a coma. Bart approached Julie, who was talking to Jay. Chase saw Julie nod to Bart, then he moved away after handing her something small.

She saw Eddie Heath with a knot of former jocks, some of whom had let their football muscles turn to quite a bit of fat. She avoided being in that part of the gym.

Out of the corner of her eye, she also kept track of Ron North. He stayed near the punch bowl, talking with classmates as they visited it. She saw him in serious conversation, or so it looked, with the man who had been principal all this time, Mr. Snelson. He was a tall, imposing man, which had served him well as principal. He was also recognizable in a crowd because of his shock of snowy white hair. An older man, shorter and dumpier, wearing a vest that was too short to meet his belt, accompanied Snelson. Ron talked and gestured to both of them. He also splashed his bourbon into their drinks successfully.

The shorter man said something and angrily waved his hands, then walked away. The next time Chase noticed, Snelson had also left Ron. She spotted his snowy hair and saw the two men on the other side of the room talking with the monarch of the night, Richard "Dickie" "Rich" Byrd. Those three hung out at the foot of the stage, laughing and joking, three good friends to all appearances. Dickie's voice still rose above the others, but Chase couldn't make out what he was saying. The other two shushed him. He looked around, then lowered his volume considerably. Chase wondered if the other man was on the school board with Dickie.

Monique Byrd was the next person to visit the punch bowl. Ron North leered at her the way he'd done at Julie, but Monique took care of him quickly. After shaking her head a few times and pointing to her husband, Dickie, she splashed her cup of punch in Ron's face with a dramatic fling of her arm.

Most of the conversation in the gym stopped. Bart Fender started toward Ron. Chase thought maybe he was going to do something physical, and he was big enough to hurt scrawny little Ron North.

But Ron headed for the door.

Chase saw Bart follow him a few minutes later. They must have both gone home because neither of them came back. She noticed that Monique and Dickie were gone, too.

One and two at a time, Chase's classmates started to leave the party. It was breaking up early. It was only a little after eleven. She looked around for Julie, but she wasn't in the room. She'd been with Jay the last time she'd seen her. The punch was horrible, but Chase was thirsty, so she headed to the table to get some more of it. Julie was there now. She smiled at Chase, then turned to address the crowd.

"Does anyone know who this belongs to?" she shouted. Julie waved a small notebook in the air. "It was here, by the punch bowl."

Chase saw Julie pick up something else, look at it, then set it down.

Nobody claimed it, but more than half the people had left by then.

Julie walked over to Chase and showed her a business card for Bart Fender. It seemed he was selling diet supplements on the side.

"Why do I want this?" Chase asked.

"There, on the other side. He wrote down Dillon Yardley's hospital room number. He said she would like some visitors."

"I thought she was in a coma."

"Me, too. It was strange." Julie turned to talk to another classmate.

Then it happened, the thing Chase dreaded. Heading toward her was Eddie Heath.

FOUR

"Chase, you look fantastic."

She glanced around, but there was no retreat. She was next to the wall that held the folded bleachers.

"I mean it. You're a sight for sore eyes."

She smiled politely and lied. "It's good to see you, too."

This jerk had dumped her a week before senior prom and she had ended up spending prom night in the corner with the other single girls, without a corsage on her wrist, watching him dance with the homecoming queen all night. Here she was without a date fourteen years later, too.

She had liked dating Eddie. After all, he was a star football *and* basketball player. He developed muscles and a beard a year before any of the other guys. She was one of the studious kids, not interested in sports—until a sports star asked her out.

The truth was, she'd had a crush on him for years before and was floating on a cloud the whole time they dated. Until he shoved her off the cloud and sent her crashing to the dirt.

"I've thought a lot about you over the years," he said.

There was no reply to that. She wouldn't admit she thought of him from time to time, too.

"I can't believe how badly I treated <u>you</u>." He grabbed her hand.

She froze. Sparks shot up her arm and hit her square in the heart. Nothing like this had ever happened with Mike Ramos. Her lips parted. She suddenly longed to kiss Eddie Heath.

Maybe because he had matured early, he had never gotten very tall. He had made his way onto the basketball team by being an excellent player. Now he tended toward short and stocky, but, oh my goodness, he still had all those rippling muscles. And those bedroom eyes.

"Can I make it up to you sometime?"

"Uh . . . when?" Yes, yes, you can. Anytime.

"Tell you what. Here's my number." He let go of her hand and Chase felt like the lights had gone out. Her shoulders sagged.

Eddie wrote his cell number on the back of a business card and handed it to her.

"You're . . . the owner of this place?"

"Yep, all mine."

The card had the words "Health from the Heath Bar" embossed in shiny green letters, with "Edward Heath, Proprietor" beneath.

"What exactly is it?"

"A health food bar."

"I guess we both own bars, then."

Chase realized she had never had business cards made. "Come by some time and I'll show you our place."

"Our?"

"I own the business with my partner, Anna Larson." She told him where Bar None was located.

Eddie flashed her a brilliant smile. "It's a deal. Give me a call."

Deal, she thought, weak in the knees.

"Am I forgiven?" Mike walked backward in front of Chase and Quincy. "I really had forgotten all about the convention. And it's one of those things that I had to go to."

Chase bent to Quincy's level. "Do you think this harness is too tight?" Right this moment she didn't want to talk about him standing her up. She woke up thinking about Eddie Heath, after all.

"It's supposed to be snug," the veterinarian said.

Chase was also a bit cranky because she didn't actually want to walk Quincy in a harness. She was only doing it to get Anna off her back. She'd been harping on it for a long time. Anna thought Quincy should get some fresh air, but not by running off, as he usually did. She thought that if he got out on a nice leashed walk, he wouldn't want to escape so much. Chase doubted that.

However, Mike Ramos, as Quincy's vet, supported Anna. So Chase finally gave in, bought a cat harness at the pet store, returned it because it was too small, bought another one, and was now taking her cat on his maiden stroll. It was Sunday, the morning after the reunion, so Mike wasn't working. Chase's shop was open, but Anna had urged her to take the walk with Mike, knowing how upset she had been that she had to go alone to the gathering.

Chase took off her gloves and fiddled with the buckles a bit, not wanting the harness to be so tight on Quincy, then stood up and continued toward Marcy Park. They wended their way west on SE Seventh Street.

"Did you have a good time?" Mike asked. "You went with Julie, right?"

"Julie and Jay. I felt like a third wheel, if you want to know." Their breath puffed clouds in the below-freezing air. The brilliant sun made the day crisp and bright, even though its warmth couldn't be felt this time of year.

"But were some people you wanted to see there?"

"Yes, and some I didn't." *And one person I thought I didn't want to see, but really did—Eddie Heath.* She wouldn't mention Eddie, though.

Quincy had been wearing the harness a little each day, to get him used to it, and he didn't seem to mind it. However, he'd been reluctant to walk out the door with it on. Chase had run upstairs to get some Go Go Balls and rolled some in front of him to get him going.

By the time they reached the corner of the park, Quincy was moving along nicely. He loved the Go Go Balls that Inger had invented for him. They were full of tuna and catnip. A few piles of fallen leaves nestled at the curbs for the next street cleaner. The world, in Minneapolis, anyway, was getting ready for winter.

Chase could hear the squeals of children on the playground, climbing and sliding and swinging. Quincy flattened his ears at the sound.

The striped cat struggled with the harness. He was able to detect that one of the clips wasn't properly seated. He was also terrified of the screaming children. There were bushes straight ahead. He should be able to slip out of the horrible contraption and hide in the bushes. He had to get away from those noises. He contorted his body and the thing snapped open.

"Oh no, there he goes," Chase cried. She shook the harness that she was left holding. "Maybe I can entice him to come out."

The bushes he had fled into were dense. There could be all kinds of bugs in there, she knew. She wasn't about to crawl into the undergrowth. It would be better if he would come out by himself.

She opened the baggie of Go Go Balls and tossed one into the growth.

"Quincy?" she called. "Quincy Wincy?"

"I'll try," Mike said, getting onto his hands and knees. "He probably won't want to stay there. There's nothing to eat."

That was true, thought Chase. Only one little Go Go Ball.

She pulled some more of them from the baggie and scattered them on the pavement.

Mike pushed the branches aside and crawled a few steps, then quickly backed out. "Call the police." His face was grim.

Chase bent down to peer into the undergrowth. Mike put his hand on her arm. "No, you don't want to look at that."

Her eyes widened. "What is it? A dead animal?"

"No, it's a dead human."

"Are you sure the person is dead?" She dove into the bushes in case they could revive whoever it was.

It was dark and dank inside the bushes. But she could see clearly. Quincy squatted on the other side of the body. It was Ron North, and he was definitely dead. It looked like he had been strangled with Julie's scarf. Quincy had raked some peanuts from Ron's pocket and was crunching them.

Chase crawled out as quickly as she could and threw up in a nearby bush while Mike dialed 911.

Ron North.

Dead.

Julie's scarf.

Oh no.

FIVE

Hours later, after Chase had let Anna know she wouldn't be at the shop anytime soon, after the crime scene technicians had left, and after she and Mike had answered countless questions over and over, Chase sat on the curb next to Mike. The yellow tape fluttered a dozen feet away. Traffic was still being routed down another street, so the rumble of cars was distant. The children were no longer on the playground. Worried parents had grabbed them all and taken them home as soon as the first police car showed up.

Detective Niles Olson hadn't come to the scene, but Chase had no doubt the homicide detective would get involved. When Quincy and Chase found dead bodies in the past—only two, though—the good-looking policeman with those impossibly dark blue eyes always turned up on the case.

"I don't have the energy to walk home," Chase said.

"You want me to get my car? My condo isn't far from here."

Chase shook her head. "No, I'm exaggerating. I'll make it. That was grueling, though." She giggled, inappropriately. "Grueling grilling, right? At least neither of us is a suspect." Her thoughts returned to Julie's scarf and what its presence at the crime scene implied.

Mike slipped an arm around her shoulder and gave her a squeeze. "Bad luck follows that cat, doesn't it? He's not even black."

Chase leaned into him, grateful he was here, next to her, at this awful time. Quincy sat next to Chase, his harness securely fastened this time. He wrapped his tail around his front feet to keep them warm.

"He's been extremely patient, hasn't he?" she said.

"Considering that, on a normal day, he probably sleeps fifteen to twenty hours, this isn't that much of a disruption."

"Except there's been a lot of commotion." She stroked his soft back. He arched it to meet her hand and purred his appreciation. "Poor little Quince. I'd better get you home."

"You should get to work, shouldn't you?"

"Gosh, yes. I hope they haven't needed me too much. I'm sure the Bar None is busy today." Saturdays and Sundays were always busy, and, nearing the holidays, business picked up more and more every weekend.

Mike stood and gave Chase a hand up. "You called Anna, but have you called Julie?"

"I need to figure out what to say." How could she tell her that her scarf had been used to strangle Ron North?

Mike gave her a curious look, probably wondering why she couldn't tell everything to her best friend, and they walked away from the park. At the point where Mike could veer off and head to his condo, Chase insisted she would go the rest of the way to the Bar None by herself. It was only a few more blocks.

As soon as Chase walked into the kitchen through the back door, Anna ran to her and gave her a hug. "What happened? You said you had to answer some questions for the police? What kind of questions? You've been gone for hours."

Chase sagged onto a stool, propped her elbows on the counter, and stuck her chin on her hands. Anna knelt to take Quincy's harness off. "How did he do?" she asked. "And I want to hear all about the reunion. Julie's told me a little bit, but—"

Chase raised an eyebrow at her pet. "He found another body."

"He *what*? You didn't say anything about a body." Anna perched on the stool next to Chase and smoothed the younger woman's hair with a worn, wrinkled hand. It felt warm and wonderful to Chase. Anna must have been baking, because the gentle scent of vanilla wafted from her.

"I couldn't talk about it right then on the phone. A man was strangled and was left in the bushes at Marcy Park. Quincy, of course, wouldn't leave it alone. Probably because Ron's pockets are . . . were . . . always stuffed with peanuts. You know Quincy and food."

Julie came out of the bathroom.

"I didn't know you were here," Chase said. She realized

she'd heard the toilet flush and the water running. She had assumed either Inger or Mallory were there.

"Anna said you were having a problem and I came over to help out."

"Was it a homeless person?" Anna asked.

"Was what a homeless person?" Julie said.

"No, it's Ron North." Chase said.

"You know him?" Anna said.

"Ron North? What about him?" Julie's voice was soft.

In high school, Julie hadn't told very many people how distraught she was by Ron's stalking. She had kept it from Anna, telling only Chase and another best friend, who moved away right after high school. Even with Chase, Julie hadn't liked to say his name. They called him The Stalking Guy.

Chase told Anna and Julie now about how he'd been killed, but failed to mention that the weapon was Julie's scarf. She could only imagine what Julie would think when she heard that. She hadn't told the police that she knew who the scarf belonged to either but knew she would have to eventually. She shuddered, picturing the disappointment in Detective Olson's eyes when he found she'd concealed that fact. She must tell him very soon. Meanwhile, she had a business to help run.

In her apartment above the Bar None shop that evening, she decided to go over everything she could remember about the reunion. Something was tickling the recesses of her consciousness. Something about that scarf.

She snuggled in her bed with a cup of chamomile tea, propped up with three down pillows. Quincy stretched out

FAT CAT TAKES THE CAKE

beside her, lying along her hips and chest. Later he would usually curl up behind her knees, after she turned onto her side. She closed her eyes, inhaling the aroma of the tea, and cast her mind back to the reunion.

Ron North had hung around the punch bowl, accosting everyone who came to get a cup. The first person Chase had talked to had been Bart Fender, when she hadn't yet seen Ron. Then Jay left with some guys to talk about football. That's when Ron came over, when Chase and Julie were alone at the punch bowl table.

He'd started accusing Julie of having something to do with a recent real estate scandal. She remembered that he'd seemed belligerent, enough so that Jay noticed and came over to get rid of Ron.

Bingo! She remembered what had been bothering her. Ron had grabbed Julie's scarf after she shoved him, then stuffed it into his own pocket when Jay scared him off. He had bothered others, too. For now, she knew enough to let herself relax. Ron had left with the scarf. Chase had finished the tea and her eyelids were drooping. She pushed two of the pillows away and nestled down to try to sleep. She had just dropped off when Julie called.

"Did the police question you?" Julie asked.

"What? About . . . Ron North?" She was going to say "finding the body" but she was unwilling to depersonalize him that much. Nor had she told Julie she was the person who had found the body.

"They're hung up on something, but they wouldn't say what. For some reason, they think I had a good reason to kill him. Detective Olson called me into the station as I was about to go to Hilda Bjorn's house to talk to her about that offer on her house." She sounded exasperated, but not frightened.

Chase guessed what they were hung up on. Somehow, they knew the scarf was Julie's. Of course, anyone who had been at the reunion might have been able to tell them that. She didn't tell Julie that she had recognized her scarf, but she would have to admit that to the detective.

Monday morning, Chase got her chance to talk to the police. Detective Olson woke her up early, wanting her to come to the station to give a formal statement. She had hoped to sleep in, since the shop was closed on Mondays and Tuesdays. She had fallen asleep, planning on telling the police how the scarf got to be with Ron North. The murderer had used it because it was there, she assumed.

She would have to say that it was Julie's. It seemed the police already knew, but if they hadn't found out yet, they would discover it sooner or later. She knew Julie hadn't killed the man, but she didn't want any suspicion to fall on her. If they knew how it got there, that should clear Julie. She hoped.

She showered and dressed in a hurry, tossed food in Quincy's bowl and freshened his water. Taking a peek at the litter box, she decided it could wait until she got back from the police station.

It was another pristine winter day. A bit warmer than Sunday. There was a tang in the air that heralded much colder weather soon. Chase hoped it wouldn't be too soon.

A parking place opened up as she pulled into the lot in

front of the imposing Second Precinct building. Careful to push the right fob button to lock her car with her gloves on, she puffed out a steamy breath of anticipation and nervousness.

She enjoyed the sun's warmth on her shoulders as she walked across the lot to the Eastside Guardian statue. She loved wearing her winter sweaters, but would rather enjoy the rare string of sunny days for longer. December in Minnesota could be a gloomy, cloudy affair. She gave the statue child's head a rub for good luck. The child gazed up, trustingly, to the policeman statue holding her bronze hand in his. Another officer in an old-fashioned dress uniform stood on the plinth beside them.

Chase hadn't decided yet exactly how she would word things to Detective Olson. Since awakening, she'd gone back and forth with herself about what she would say. She had to make sure he knew Julie couldn't have killed Ron. The words to "Follow Your Heart" floated through her head. Anna had never taken her to a performance of *Urinetown*, disliking the name of the musical intensely, but Chase had heard the lyrics plenty of places.

She told herself she had better decide soon. Squaring her shoulders, she yanked open the large wooden door and went to meet her fate.

After she gave her statement, telling about Quincy getting away and Dr. Ramos crawling in to retrieve him, and then about her recognizing the victim, she signed the printout the detective handed her. She had repeated what she had said yesterday and hadn't mentioned the scarf yet. But she would. Soon.

"I need to show you some things now," he said. He opened a folder that held large color photos.

The first picture Detective Olson showed her was of the scarf. Her heart sank.

"Do you recognize this?" He shoved the photo toward her across his desk. His desk sat in the middle of several rows of them in the large room. The policeman beside them clacked his computer keys, typing with two fingers and bobbling his head between his monitor and his keyboard. Chase wondered if he would have a headache later.

"Yes." She swallowed. "I saw it by the body."

"Have you ever seen it before?" He raised his eyebrows and looked at her sideways.

"Yes." It was time to fess up. "It belongs to Julie Larson. Ron took it from her at the reunion."

"He took her scarf?" Now he looked like he didn't believe her. "Why would he do that?"

Oh dear. She had to be careful to not implicate Julie. There had been a mini-scene and surely some of the people there had seen it. "He was talking to her and . . . took hold of it."

"That's odd. Were they arguing?"

"Not really arguing." She reached up to twist a lock of her hair, then clasped her hands in her lap. No nervous gestures, she told herself. "They were talking."

"What about?"

"He was getting drunk. He tried to pour some bourbon into her punch." That would have improved the nasty too-sweet stuff, but she didn't say that. "Julie told Ron she didn't want any bourbon. He started pouring it in her cup anyway.

She jerked her cup away and he spilled some from his own flask."

"I see." Olson leaned back in his chair, implying that he saw more than what Chase was saying.

Chase thought she was making a mess of this. "Ron was bothering a lot of people at the reunion. He's an annoying person."

"Did he bother you?"

"Not really."

"Just Julie."

"He used to have a thing for her. In high school."

Niles Olson's blue eyes sparked as he leaned forward again and rested his forearms on his desk. "A thing. What kind of thing?"

Yes, she was making things worse and worse. "It was a long time ago." She waved her hand, carelessly, she hoped. "You know, a high school crush."

"Uh huh." He jotted something down on a yellow pad. "Who else did he tangle with at the reunion?"

"He didn't 'tangle with' Julie. They . . . talked." And he mashed her face into his for an unwelcome kiss. She realized she was now twisting the strands of her straight brown-blonde hair. She put her hand down again. "He went up to quite a few people. He talked to our old principal, Mr. Snelson. And some other older man who was with Mr. Snelson. They both argued with Ron. And he talked to Monique. Oh yes, Monique threw her punch in his face. I just remembered."

He was writing as she talked. "Anyone else?"

"Probably, but I'd have to think some more. He left soon after Monique did that. Can I go now?"

He nodded and she fled.

All the way home she worried that she hadn't mentioned Ron literally stalking Julie in high school. She probably should have. His latest victim seemed to be Monique, though. She had also omitted the kiss Ron forced on Julie. Would their altercation make Julie look more guilty? Or less? If Chase knew, she would know what to say to the police.

A text popped up on her phone as she stopped for a red light. She grabbed her cell and quickly read the message from Julie: "Where are you?" The light changed before she could reply.

Pulling into the parking lot behind her apartment and shop, she saw Julie sitting in her pickup, clouds of vapor streaming out of the tailpipe, glittering in the sunlight, as she ran the engine to keep warm. Julie spotted Chase right away, turned off the engine, and jumped out.

Anna's car was there, too, beside Julie's truck.

"Anna's here? Why aren't you inside?"

"I just got here. Grandma's working on her recipe," Julie said. "I offered to help, but she would rather do it alone. Where have you been?"

"At the police station to give my statement. They got it yesterday, kind of, but I had to sign it today."

Julie didn't ask if her name had come up and Chase didn't mention it.

They headed for the door, chatting about Anna. "She turned in the recipe, right?" Chase said. "What is she working on now?"

"She's practicing making it, over and over."

"We'll have lots of her new bars to sell on Wednesday, I guess, if she'll let us."

They both poked their heads into the kitchen to say hi to Anna, inhaled nosefuls of the heavenly blueberry aroma, then ran upstairs for some hot chocolate.

"What was that about the real estate deal?" Chase asked. "What was Ron North talking about?" Should she mention the scarf?

Julie blew on her cocoa. "That's a bad deal. You know I told you about someone offering Hilda Bjorn way too little for her house? I dropped by this morning to ask her about it. She described the man who came to her door." Julie shook her head.

"And?"

"Who does this sound like? She said he had a commanding presence and very nice snowy white hair. Like an egret, she said."

"Principal Snelson? Why would he be trying to make a real estate deal?"

Julie shrugged. "Do you know who that other guy was Saturday night? The short one?"

"Never saw him before. He's not our age; must be a friend of Snelson's."

"Almost forgot." Julie pulled a small black notebook from her purse as they sat sipping at Chase's kitchen table. "I have to show you this."

"What is it?" Chase asked, setting her mug down and taking the notebook from her. The handwriting was small and cramped.

"I found it by the punch bowl Saturday night. Remember? I asked around and no one said it was theirs."

"Yes, I remember. You waved it around. It was after Ron and some others left."

They stared at each other, realization dawning.

In unison, they said, "It's Ron's!"

SIX

J ulie and Chase spent another few minutes going over the
happenings at the reunion together. They decided they
couldn't be completely sure it was Ron's, since so many others were gone when Julie found it. But Chase thought it was
very much like the notebook he had whipped out in the Bar
None days ago, hoping to interview her. She couldn't be
positive, though. It was nondescript, a small spiral-bound
booklet with a black cover.

"Well, we'd better look inside," Julie said, turning it over
and over with her fingertips, like she was reluctant to
touch it too much.

"That's not illegal or anything?"

"How else can we find out who it belongs to?"

Many of the pages were filled with small, barely legible

writing. They were, as far as she could tell, notes for stories Ron had been working on. Words that they could read stood out. Amid several references to "school board" were the words "real estate." Chase found her name with a reminder to the author to get "pix of Bar None" developed. "This has to be Ron's. This is what he was working on."

Julie flipped through to the end and was confronted by gibberish.

"Here," Chase said, turning the book upside down. "He's started some notes from the back. He's using the front part for notes on his stories."

"Ah. Writing from front to back and also from back to front. But what is this?"

Three words were written at the top of the page, one to a line: PRINCE, PHOTO, and BIRD. The first two words were repeated below on many lines, and were accompanied by dates with numbers after them. This went on for two and half pages. The word BIRD wasn't repeated.

"Is it a code?" Chase asked.

"He was a reporter. Does it have something to do with articles and photographs?"

Chase drummed her fingers on the table. "Dates and numbers. Are those three horses he bet on?"

"He never bet on the BIRD horse, if they are." Julie thumbed on from the back until she came to some more pages with writing. "Here are some more notations."

These entries were even more cryptic. Each line had an initial followed by a date.

"Why are these in pink ink?" Chase wondered. "The other stuff before this is all in blue."

"Boys and girls?"

Chase took a good look at the dates. They went back several years. Most of the earlier initials were J, with D and M occurring both there and more recently. After those first entries, a few more were listed: L, K, and Q. Beside the bottom M was the date Ron North had been in her dessert bar shop. She put her finger on that line.

"Here. Look at this. Ron and Monique were both in my shop this day. She was uncomfortable being around him, too."

The last entry held both an M and a J and the date of the reunion. The J was in light pencil rather than pink ink.

"He wrote down the dates he saw Monique? That's weird."

Chase put her finger on the J. "That's you, Julie. This is his stalking log."

Julie shivered. "A ghost just walked up my spinal column. I wonder if you're right."

"And Monique. He bothered her that night, too."

They spent nearly an hour poring over the notebook, but made no headway with the blue entries, except to assume they referred to men and not women.

Julie jumped up. "I gotta go. I need to figure out some things on a case this afternoon. Plus, I have to work tomorrow, unlike some people I know. Unless I get questioned one more time. Detective Olson said they might want to talk to me again." Her voice tightened on that last sentence.

Chase didn't like the sound of that either. She gave her friend a long hug.

Julie paused before she walked out the door. "Wait a sec." She closed her eyes. "I saw our principal hand something to Ron when they were standing together."

"Did you see what it was?"

"No, but Mr. Snelson wasn't happy about it."

"So, if he's one of these people in blue, did the handoff have something to do with the amounts?"

"Payment for something, maybe. Drugs?"

"Mr. Snelson, our principal? I guess it's possible. This could be a blackmail scheme." suggested Chase.

They looked at each other and shrugged.

"Why don't you make me a copy of that?" Julie said. "I'd like to go over it some more."

They both traipsed downstairs to use the copy machine.

After Julie left, Chase—disappointed that Anna was gone—did some dusting and some laundry, and worried some more about Julie. She eventually fell asleep on her couch, staring at the last few pages of the notebook. She knew they would have to give it to the police. Julie was in enough trouble without withholding evidence. She would make another copy of the notebook for herself first thing in the morning in the office downstairs.

The shop was closed on Tuesdays, but Chase took the notebook downstairs to make her own copy as soon as she was dressed. Quincy had the run of the shop, something he enjoyed whenever he got a chance.

Chase heard a commotion at the back door and ran to find Anna carrying in a heavy-looking grocery bag.

"More baking today?" Chase asked, taking the burden from her. "We're going to have tons of your new creation to sell on Wednesday."

"No, we're not," Anna said, handing the heavy bag to Chase and returning to her blue Volvo to fetch a couple more off the rear seat. She was on her way back before Chase could follow her out to help. "I'm only doing parts of the recipe. I'm not finishing anything."

"That's too bad." Chase had been looking forward to helping sample them. "Do you have any more bags?"

"This is it."

Chase shivered in the doorway waiting for Anna to return.

"I have to get good enough so that every step goes as smoothly as possible. Part of my score will depend on how quickly I work. During the competition, I'd like to be flawless. Or as near as a human can get."

Chase pecked Anna on the cheek as she returned to the warm kitchen. "You already are nearly perfect, dear Anna."

"Oh, go on." Anna smiled as she started extracting baking supplies from the bags and strewing them onto the granite counter.

"Wait. Before you get started, I'd like to show you something. Did Julie tell you about what she found at the reunion?"

"I guess not." Anna shook her head in puzzlement.

Chase ran into the office to get the notebook.

The cat, left in the office alone, set out to declutter the desktop. An offensive object sat on the corner. It was small and black. The cat batted it to the floor. That didn't seem to satisfy him, though. A loose sheet had fallen out. He shoved the extra piece until it was out of sight underneath

the desk. He had nearly gotten the notebook there, too, when his mistress came into the office.

"Now where is that thing?" Chase's eyes searched her desk, then her toe kicked the notebook. "Oh, I'll bet you cleaned off the desk, didn't you?" She gave Quincy a head rub and took the notebook into the kitchen to show Anna.

"What do you make of this?" she asked.

Anna leafed through it, puzzling over the arcane notations. "Do you have any idea what these pertain to? Are PRINCE and PHOTO and BIRD the names of . . . animals, people?"

"I haven't figured it out. They're things, right? One is a person, one is an object, and one is an animal."

Anna handed her the notebook. "You got me." She frowned and shrugged, then started setting out ingredients for her Batter Battle creation.

"We think we might know what some of the things in pink mean." She explained what Julie and she had figured out about the stalking dates and initials.

"Charity, I have to keep practicing until I don't make any mistakes. I'm not nearly there yet and I don't have time for games."

At Chase's shocked expression, Anna softened. "I'm sorry. I know a man is dead and this isn't a game to you. But if you don't know what anything means, those writings are useless. I'm sure the police can figure it out. Don't they have experts to do that kind of thing? You say Julie found it. Why do you have it now?"

"I ended up with it. Wouldn't it look better for me to turn it in than Julie? I don't want them to suspect her any more than they already do."

"I'm sure they'll get to the truth, find out who did what, and won't blame Julie for anything."

Although Chase didn't hold out much hope for that—after all, Niles Olson wasn't familiar with any of these people—she hoped Anna was right. The next thing she had to do, after she copied the pages, was to give the notebook to Detective Olson.

SEVEN

The rest of Tuesday, Chase's second day off, was jam-packed. She dropped the notebook off at the front desk of the police station—Detective Olson wasn't in, to her relief. She didn't want to explain to him where the notebook had been until now.

Today she absolutely had to buy shoes. Unlike Julie and Anna, she took no delight in that exercise. Those two put together a strategy days in advance and planned their shoe excursions like battles. Chase merely shopped for footwear when she had to. And her sneakers had a hole in the toe. It was time.

She needed wedding shoes, too, but had to get those with Julie along so they would match. At least she was spared shopping for gifts for Julie and Anna this year. They had decided, with the wedding and the busy season at the shop, not to give one another anything for Christmas.

Before sneaker shopping, she decided to take Quincy out for some more leash training. She needed to train herself on how to attach the harness, too, so that he wouldn't slip out of it when she left a strap unfastened. It didn't take much for that little guy to figure out where the weaknesses were. She didn't expect more dead bodies, but it wouldn't do for him to get loose on a sidewalk and run into the street.

She made sure the harness was snug and all the fasteners were in place. Getting Quincy out the back door required a bit of coaxing. That figures, she thought. If the door were left open a quarter of an inch, he'd be sneaking through it in a heartbeat. But make it easy for him, and he didn't want to budge. They made it into the parking lot and proceeded toward the sidewalk, passing through the shade of a tree planted at the corner.

Chase decided to turn south, toward the river. She looked up and down SE Fourth Street when they reached it to see if any large dogs lurked. Or any small dogs, for that matter.

Her least favorite politico stood outside a small bar half a block away. She had no desire to speak to him, to have to lie about why his campaign poster wasn't in the window of the Bar None, so she turned away and walked the other direction.

Then what she'd seen registered and she did a double take. Dickie Byrd wasn't looking in her direction at all. His gaze was glued to the face of the woman in his arms. She sure wasn't his wife, Mona. Chase couldn't help herself. She stopped, dumbfounded. She watched as Dickie bent toward the woman and their lips met. Quincy twined around her legs, not wanting to stop now that they were on their way.

The woman was a lot shorter than Mona, and a lot more stacked. Where Mona was delicate, fluttery, this woman was solid. Even accounting for her down jacket, she was heftier than Dickie's model-slim wife. And she had no qualms about extra-long and passionate public kisses.

Chase pulled herself away and walked on. Quincy trotted with her happily. Moving was better than standing still in this weather. And here Chase had thought Dickie might be a suspect in Ron North's death, defending his wife's honor from her stalker. Not hardly! He was wadding up his wife's honor and kicking it to the curb.

She might as well circle around and head north to Hilda Bjorn's house and check on the woman. From the information Julie had, she thought Ms. Bjorn had described the principal as the man who made the very low offer on her house. That made no sense.

Chase was glad the real estate case was taking Julie's mind off the murder investigation. At least, she hoped it was.

Quincy bounded up the few steps to Hilda's front porch. He knew and liked the old woman. A small, vibrant woman in her late eighties, dressed in a blue velour pantsuit, opened the door. Her wire-rim glasses winked in the frosty sunshine and her face wrinkled with joy.

"Two of my favorites! Come in, Chase. Come in, Quincy. Let me see what I can rustle up for you."

Chase followed her into the small, snug living room. "Please don't, Ms. Bjorn. We have only a few minutes." Not quite true, but she didn't want the woman stuffing Quincy with tuna fish or, worse, cookies. "I would like to ask you about the man who offered you some money for your house. My friend Julie Larson told me a little bit about it. She's working on this for her real estate office."

"My, there are a lot of people involved, aren't there? Well, it's a great deal of money."

"How much exactly did he say?"

"He said at least twenty thousand!"

"You know, that's not very much for this house. It's a desirable neighborhood. If you do want to sell, you could probably get a lot more."

"Oh, but Mr. Nelson said I had to make up my mind quickly or the offer would go down."

"Mr. Nelson?"

"Yes, I remembered his name this morning because I had a boyfriend named Vance once. His name is Vance."

Vance? "Did he show you his real estate credentials?"

"Oh, you sound just like Professor Fear. He's very suspicious of this nice man. I can't imagine why. I didn't think to do that. He looks honest."

A knock sounded on the door and Ms. Bjorn let Professor Anderson Fear into the living room. Chase glimpsed his blue fat-tire bike leaned against her porch railing. He peered at Chase, then took off his steamy glasses and wiped them on the tail of his plaid shirt. As usual, his hair stuck up in places and his clothing was rumpled and disheveled. Exactly right for a professor, Chase thought.

"We were talking about you, Andy, this very minute. I'll get you some hot chocolate." Ms. Bjorn bustled out of the room to her kitchen.

"Chase Oliver," the man said, finally placing who she was. "Do you know how soon your friend Ms. Larson can talk to both of us?"

"I know that she's taking this pro bono, so has to squeeze visits in. She was here yesterday, but you must have missed her. Ms. Bjorn was telling me about the guy who made the offer to her."

"I guess I missed seeing her," Professor Fear said.

Hilda Bjorn came back with a steaming mug for the professor.

"You're not having any?" he asked Chase.

"No, we have to get going. But you go ahead. You're probably cold from your bike ride."

He perched on the edge of the couch cushion, which sagged halfway to the floor with his slight weight. "It's not that cold yet. It's above zero. Did you tell Chase about the man? What was his name?"

"Vance," Ms. Bjorn said.

"What does he look like?" Chase asked.

"A great big egret, one of those white ones. A snowy egret."

"Is he tall, short?"

"No, more medium height, I think. He was very nice."

"Ms. Bjorn, please promise me that you'll talk to Professor Fear before you sign anything. Make sure you do that, okay?"

"Yes, Hilda," he said. "Don't sign anything at all unless I'm there."

"All right, but I think you young people are being too suspicious."

"Maybe we are, but it's better to be safe," Chase said, and headed out.

Hilda Bjorn closed the door after them, clucking, and shaking her head. In general, Chase thought Ms. Bjorn was on the ball, but her idea of house prices was stuck in the year that she bought hers and was sadly out of date. Just the thing an unscrupulous land broker would count on.

Then it clicked. Van Snelson? Heard as Vance Nelson. Mr. Snelson, however, was not a land broker. He was a high school principal. She would talk to Julie about all this again tonight when Jules was off work. And she must remember to mention seeing Dickie Byrd with—whoever that was. Right out there on a public sidewalk. Did the man have no sense of self-preservation, what with his election coming up? He had never gotten academic honors in high school, but he had won elections. Was there such a thing as being election-smart and not smart-smart?

Rounding the last corner to the parking lot behind the Bar None, Chase was surprised to see Eddie Heath leaning against a bright yellow Smart car. He broke into a glowing smile when he saw her coming.

He waved, so Chase returned the gesture. But she wondered what he was doing here, behind the shop. It was closed today, so he probably wouldn't find out where she'd gone from anyone inside. Anna was still here, as evidenced by her blue Volvo. She didn't usually answer the door when she was alone, though.

"Nobody answered your doorbell when I tried it," he shouted. "I was about to leave when I saw you."

When she got near, she greeted Eddie. "Hi. We've been on a walk. Did you need some dessert bars?"

"Nope." He grinned again.

"That's good, because we're closed today. But I could get some if you're interested."

"I'm more interested in the shop owner right now."

He was flirting with her! Her high school crush had come around to see her after the reunion. She was conscious of a faint blush spreading up from her neck as she recalled the tingle she'd felt when they touched that night. "Are you . . . are you here for the tour I promised you?"

"Maybe. But I thought I could buy you lunch first."

Was he going to apologize for dumping her right before their high school prom? No, Chase, she told herself. Don't bring that up. It's water under the bridge.

"Have you eaten?" he asked.

"No. Sure, I'd like that. I'll be out in a minute."

She scooped Quincy up and ran up the stairs to deposit him in the apartment. She wet her hands and patted her hair into place, then ran a tinted gloss over her lips. Then, for good measure, even though she knew she was about to eat, she swished some mouthwash.

As she checked her teeth in the mirror, Mike Ramos's face popped up in her mind. This wasn't a date, she told the imaginary Mike, it was merely getting together with an old classmate. *Who I bumped into when I went to the reunion without you. Because you finked out at the last minute.*

Crossing her fingers, she hoped going to lunch with Eddie Heath wasn't the wrong thing to do.

EIGHT

Chase let Eddie pick the restaurant and he drove her to an out-of-the-way place. The outside of Gourmet Leaves and Plants was interesting and even funky. When they got seated Eddie started enthusing over the menu.

"See this?" He pointed to the top of the sheet. "Organic. Vegan. Raw. Gluten-free."

Chase suppressed a shudder. "Is there regular food, too?" The weather was chilly and she had been looking forward to some thick, creamy soup, or maybe a juicy hamburger.

Eddie flashed that grin. "This *is* regular food. What's wrong with it?"

Chase saw the selection of chilled soups. Nothing hot. "Well, are there any burgers?" She flipped the menu over, searching in vain for some comfort food. There were an awful lot of juices listed.

"Let me order. I promise you'll love it. This place serves only healthy food."

The waiter was hovering by them now. Eddie told him they would both start with a "rejuvenator."

Chase started to look for it on the menu, then decided not to. She would give it a chance based on the taste. When the glass arrived, she sniffed the cloudy liquid. It smelled fresh and lemony. However, when she took a sip, she barely managed to swallow it. "I think I'll need some water, too."

"You don't like the fermented quinoa sprouts?" Eddie's face fell, disappointed.

"Maybe it's the ginger." There was at least five times more of the stuff than she could take in the "rejuvenator."

The waiter was still nearby. "What kind of water?" he asked.

"Just regular water, please."

"Unflavored?"

"Tap water, please."

The waiter sniffed. "We do not serve tap water."

"Then please bring me whatever you have."

She got a glass bottle of "oxygen-infused water" that tasted rather musty, but better than the fermented quinoa.

The meal went downhill from there. Eddie had ordered her a falafel wrap that tasted good, but she would have much preferred something hot and filling.

Eddie steered the conversation to the weather and the background on almost every item from the menu. Chase was relieved that he didn't bring up anything from high school, like, the prom. She remained polite and listened to his discourse on healthy food, nodding and staying silent on the subject. After all, she was in the business of making and selling sweet treats.

While they were waiting for the check, Chase noticed the man at a table across the small dining room. He had just been ushered in and seated. A waiter was standing above him, waiting to take his order. "I'm sorry," the waiter said. "Could you repeat that?"

"I said I want a drink!"

The waiter drew himself up slightly. "Sir, we do not serve alcohol here."

"Well, what good is this place?" Chase thought he must be pretty drunk to think this place would have a bar that served anything other than juice and liquid sprouts. The man struggled to his feet. He reeled, then stumbled toward the door. He was short and stout and the vest he wore strained at the buttons over his tummy. Recognition dawned.

"Eddie," Chase whispered. "Do you know who that man is?"

Eddie squinted in the man's direction. "I've seen him somewhere."

"At the reunion. Wasn't he talking with Mr. Snelson?"

"Might have been."

Chase was sure now. That was the man who had talked with Mr. Snelson and had argued with Ron North. He was now very drunk and still trying to get more liquor. Maybe he'd been blackmailed by Ron and had killed him and was now so remorseful that he was drinking too much? Maybe her imagination was filling in too many blanks.

If only she and Julie could figure out what the entries in Ron's notebook meant!

Eddie drove her to the rear parking lot, which was where she almost always entered her shop and her apartment. He continued Chase's healthy food education on the way and she continued to bite her tongue, resisting mention of the fact that some people like food that tasted good and filled them up.

"Would you like to come in and pick out a dessert?" As soon as she'd said the words, she realized that he probably wouldn't.

"Do you have anything healthy?"

She thought about their products. She'd seen a lot of coconut oil on the menu at the vegan place. "We have Hula Bars. They're full of pineapple and coconut."

Maybe he wouldn't ask what else was in them. If he had any taste at all, he'd surely like them.

"Sounds good. Sure."

In case Anna had let Quincy loose in the kitchen, she guarded the door with her foot when she opened it. Sure enough, the cat was sitting there, looking at Anna patiently. Probably wishing she would drop something onto the floor.

Anna glanced up as they entered the toasty warm kitchen. "Who's this?" she asked with a tentative smile.

"Eddie. We went to high school together. We ran into each other today and I offered him a Hula Bar or two." And he set me on fire when we touched. I'm not really two-timing Mike Ramos. Simply getting him a Hula Bar, she thought to herself.

"Go right ahead." Anna returned to her ingredients, laid out in small bowls and dishes, but kept her eye on Chase and Eddie until they were through the swinging double doors.

Quincy followed them and Anna whispered to him, "Go ahead, Quincy. You chaperone them."

Chase suspected that Anna thought her whisper was softer than it was.

Chase flicked the lights on. "I'll show you the shop first," she said. "The only products out right now are some of the boxed treats." The glass case got emptied every night. "Would you like a box of Hula Bars?"

"Maybe I should try a taste first?"

"Go ahead and take this. Give them away if you don't like them." She shoved a box into his hands in spite of his doubtful expression. He raised his eyebrows and squinted at it. "What's in these?"

"I told you. Pineapple and coconut. Also some walnuts."

"Any sugar?"

"Brown sugar." Surely that would be all right for a health nut.

"Flour?" Quincy rubbed against Eddie's pant leg. He lowered his chin, frowned, and moved his leg slightly away from the cat.

"Of course."

He pushed the box toward her. "I can't eat white flour. You shouldn't either."

"Some of our products don't contain flour."

"How about white sugar?"

She admitted that most of them did. She wouldn't be able

69

to eat many of her own wares if she didn't eat flour or sugar. At the moment, she couldn't think of any that were up to Eddie's standards.

"When you start selling some healthy products, let me know. I'll take you to my own place next time."

She remembered the card he'd given her. Health from the Heath Bar, it had said. Wow, she was sure looking forward to another health food place. It wasn't a good name, she thought, since it made her think of a candy bar. She'd bet there wouldn't be any candy bars at any Health from the Heath Bar.

"I'll give you call," he said as she showed him out the back door.

If he didn't, maybe that would be all right since it seemed they had nothing in common now.

"What was that all about?" Anna asked after Eddie left.

"An old high school friend. I told you."

"Why are you blushing?" Anna raised her eyebrows and squinted in the same skeptical way Eddie had at her wares. "Is he an old flame?"

"Yes, with emphasis on *old*. Not anymore. I'm going to buy some new sneakers. Quincy, you be good while I'm gone." She leaned down to give him a few strokes, loving the rumbling purr he returned. She left before Anna could talk about Eddie Heath any more. She was conflicted enough without trying to explain herself to her partner.

Anna was gone when she returned with her new sneakers. She hadn't even considered asking Anna along. Although Anna loved shoe shopping, she wouldn't love trying on anything as prosaic and practical as everyday work shoes. Anna hadn't stayed to see them, so Chase knew she was right.

Julie had called her while she was trying on her fifth pair of shoes, then Chase had decided to catch a bite of supper at a fast food place near the mall. She had to have something substantial after that lunch. By the time she got back it was nearly seven.

She sipped her takeout drink through the plastic straw as she entered her apartment, greeted Quincy—Anna must have brought him here when she left—and returned Julie's call.

"Where have you been? Anyplace interesting?" Julie asked.

"I've been doing your favorite thing, buying a pair of shoes."

"Only one pair? I never buy just one."

"Well, I know, but I never buy two."

"Right. Okay, spill, what kind, what color? Where did you go?"

"They're mostly white, with some blue—"

"You bought tennis shoes! You're bragging about buying tennis shoes?"

So Julie thought as much of her purchase as Anna must have, obviously. Chase still had to buy her wedding shoes, too. She hadn't seen a thing she liked today. "Yes, I bought shoes for work. My other pair is falling apart. Now, what did you call me about?"

"Ooh, I have a scoop. I think. One of the other lawyers was talking to me in the break room about an older man who is in the process of getting his real estate license. I didn't pay much attention until he said the man is a high school principal, and has been forever."

"Mr. Snelson?" Chase toed off her old sneakers and curled up in the corner of her leather couch—her one splurge when she'd been furnishing the apartment. After Quincy inspected the new bag with the shoebox inside, he joined her and got a head scratch for his efforts.

"Mr. Van Snelson! None other. Yes, he even knew his name. Our principal is going to quit his job as soon as he qualifies, evidently. My colleague knows the woman who teaches the class he's taking. Mr. Snelson has told the teacher that he wants to keep it quiet until he's ready to make the change."

"Oh, so the teacher tells your lawyer friend, who tells you, who tells me. So much for keeping it quiet."

"How does he think no one is going to find out? It's not illegal to say who your students are. So far, though, that's only four people."

"So far. What a strange thing for him to do, don't you think? Go into real estate?"

"Eh, I don't know. He's been at that school for ages, but I don't think anyone ever liked him."

"You're not supposed to like the principal, are you?" Chase recalled, though, that she had adored her principal in grade school.

"Why not? If you're not a troublemaker, there's no reason you shouldn't get along with him."

"You and I certainly weren't troublemakers, were we?"

"Wellll," Julie drawled. "There was that time . . ."

"Oh yes, but we never got caught."

"What's that horrible noise?"

Chase had reached the bottom of her drink and had slurped. Quincy, annoyed at the racket, too, jumped down. "My drink."

"I also wanted to tell you that I was called into the police station at noon."

"How did that go, Jules?"

She took a deep breath, sounding shaky. "Not the funnest lunch hour I ever took. That Detective Olson is a grim guy."

"He can be. What did he ask you about?"

"Lots, including the fact that my scarf was used to strangle Ron North. I remember Ron took it with him, but I get the idea he doesn't believe me. I made the mistake of telling the detective it's one of my favorites, so he wanted to know why I didn't get it back. I couldn't stand dealing with Ron, is why, but Olson is not buying it. He knows about the thing in high school, too. Someone must have told him."

Chase cringed, glad Julie couldn't see her face.

"But I've been going over those pages you copied for me. I saw something I hadn't noticed before."

Shaking her new shoes out of the box, Chase left it with the lid off so Quincy could jump in and out of it. He would probably do that for at least half an hour. "Wait, let me get my copy." Chase spread the pages out on her kitchen table.

"Look at the page with those weird names."

Chase pulled the sheet toward her.

"See it? The extra letter?"

"No." She held the paper up closer to her face. "Oh, yes, I do." A faint J was written lightly below the word BIRD. "He was thinking of adding to this list? Someone named J? Has it been penciled in? I think so."

"BIRD, Chase, think of it. Isn't that Dickie Byrd?"

"Then who is PRINCE?"

"I've been thinking about that, too. I still remember how to spell principal the way our second grade teacher taught us. He's a prince of a pal, she said."

"Yes, I remember that. So you think this is the principal, Mr. Snelson?"

"Maybe. I have no idea who PHOTO is, but I'll bet these are blackmail victims. And I think I was about to be added to the list."

NINE

Chase thought, on the surface, that Julie's theory was far-fetched. She had asked her what on earth Ron North would be blackmailing her about. But when Julie pointed out that he was working on the real estate swindle story, Chase began to change her mind. Maybe he was trying to blackmail everyone involved in that. Eventually, he would have realized that Julie wasn't part of any swindle. So much for the real estate case distracting Julie from being a murder suspect.

Ron probably had a chance at shaking down whoever had offered the money to Hilda Bjorn. And that might be Mr. Snelson, since he was getting into the real estate business and there were what looked like dollar amounts next to his code name. If PRINCE *was* his code name. That would mean that Hilda Bjorn's Vance Nelson actually was Van Snelson. There were amounts written in for the person called PHOTO, too. Maybe Mr. Snelson had a partner in crime who was already certified to handle real estate.

If BIRD was Dickie Byrd, Ron North hadn't been successful at getting any money out of him. Chase leafed through Ron's story notes to find anything that might pertain to wrongdoing on the part of Dickie. It looked like Ron had started to interview the principal for an article on the school board. He seemed to suspect there were some shady activities going on there. The notes went on to mention the real estate scams. There were also notes about historical swindles, maybe to fill out his intended article.

Dickie Byrd didn't figure in those pages. However, Dickie was an easy target even if he hadn't taken part in the scams. If he was always this careless about kissing women other than his wife in public, Ron could easily try to blackmail him about his indiscretions.

Chase devoutly hoped the police could figure out Ron's code. His notes flitted from one thing to another so that she didn't know how he had planned to write anything coherent from them. She also wished, even more devoutly, that J would end up standing for someone other than Julie.

Before they had hung up, Chase had described to Julie the person she and Eddie had seen at lunch, drunk. Julie remembered him from the reunion, but had no idea who he was. Was he PHOTO?

She couldn't sleep with all of this rattling around inside her head, so she padded down to the office, leaving Quincy snoring softly on her bed.

Ron's notebook mentioned the school board, and Dickie was on it. Maybe the scandal that got him killed wasn't real estate, but something to do with the school board. She looked up the local school board and there was Dickie Byrd's picture, the same one he was using on his campaign posters. Another member stood out to her. It was the man with the vest, the short, dumpy drunk she'd seen at lunch.

His name was Langton Hail and, upon further investigation, she found he was a real estate developer. He had built hotel complexes in several major cities.

It took her a long time to fall asleep with the associations and cross-associations whirling in her poor, tired brain.

Chase was glad she would be working in the shop today to take her mind off Ron North's murder and everything else related to it.

Since the shop was fairly busy, she worked the counter beside Mallory, the new hire. About midmorning, it dawned on Chase what bothered her about Mallory. The woman, little more than a girl, rarely smiled. She knew this was her first job out of high school, but her résumé had listed an impressive number of retail places she had worked during the summers. Shortly before lunchtime there was a lull, one of those rare times without a single person in the shop.

"Mallory," Chase began, then wondered how to continue. She paused, then forged ahead. "I need to tell you something very important about selling things to people."

Mallory drew in her breath, her eyes wide with worry. "What am I doing wrong? Did I miscount the change?"

Chase gave her what she hoped was a reassuring smile. "No, nothing like that." It suddenly occurred to her that the reason Mallory's list of jobs was so long could be that she got fired from all of them. "You're doing fine, really. But, well, I'm sure you've heard that first impressions are important. Right?"

Mallory nodded, but the worry remained etched on her face. She sucked on her bottom lip and hunched her thin shoulders.

"Relax, dear. I'm going to tell you a secret. There's only one thing you need to do to improve what you're already doing. It's a tiny thing, but it makes a huge first impression. When you first interact with a customer, you smile. That's it. The customer is at ease, so you're more at ease. Things will go smoothly if they feel comfortable with you from the start."

Mallory nodded, her posture and her face losing some of the tension.

Just then, the tension in the shop kicked up one hundred percent. Grace Pilsen, Anna's old baking rival, strode into the Bar None, throwing the door open so violently that the usually soft bell jangled loudly. She looked fierce, but that was her normal expression, Chase thought. She'd never seen the woman without an angry scowl on her face.

Confronted with this new, terrifying customer, Mallory reassumed her worried expression. Chase couldn't blame her for not trying out the smile technique with this woman.

"Ms. Pilsen," Chase said, also not smiling. "Is there anything I can help you with?"

"I need to speak to Anna." She ended her sentence with an unattractive sneer. The white skunk streak in her suspiciously black hair always made Chase think of Cruella De Vil, the villain in the *One Hundred and One Dalmatians* Disney movie. A shorter, plumper version. The woman obviously ate a lot of what she baked at The Pilsener.

Anna had heard her snarling voice, which was rather loud, and came barging through the double doors almost as violently as Grace had entered the shop. The doors *whomp*ed as they swung back and forth a few times in Anna's wake.

"What do *you* want here?" Anna asked.

"I'm trying to keep you from being disqualified."

Anna drew herself up to her full height, which wasn't much more than Grace's. Both women measured about five feet tall.

They faced off in front of the sales counter, the lights of the display case below acting as spotlights on the action. Mallory and Chase watched in fascinated silence.

"I'll have you know," Anna said, "that I'm officially entered and have turned in my recipe. My paperwork is all in order."

"Except for this." Grace extracted a piece of paper from the briefcase she carried and waved it toward Anna, who came forward and grabbed it.

"This is my application. I turned this in long ago. My acceptance was based on this."

"Look at the bottom." Grace's sneer grew uglier. "You neglected to sign your full name."

Anna glanced at the sheet. "I . . . *what*?" She put her finger on the signature that even Chase could see from behind the counter.

"What kind of a signature is A. A. Larson?"

"It's my legal signature. I use it on everything."

"That's right," Chase put in. "She does."

Grace shot Chase a withering look, her upper lip curling like Elvis's. "That could mean a lot of different people. What with all the Alvas and Anderses and Arvas around here."

"Grace," Anna said. "Go home. That's my signature and anyone can compare it to hundreds of other things I've signed. Get out of my shop."

Grace drew air in through her dilated nostrils, stuffed the paper inside her briefcase, and left, torturing the bell again on her way out.

"Doesn't she have anything better to do than harass people?" Anna muttered as she returned to the kitchen.

The shop started to fill with shoppers, so Chase stayed on in front. She looked up as she was sliding some bars from the display case into a bag and saw Tanner, the kid who handled the web presence for Bar None, standing behind her customer. When the woman gathered her purchases and left, Tanner moved to the counter. This time the lights in the display case winked on his nose ring.

Mallory gave Tanner a huge grin and welcomed him to the shop. "Can I help you?"

She was learning, thought Chase, although maybe now she was being overly enthusiastic.

Tanner smiled back at Mallory, but spoke to Chase. "I came by to see what's going on with the webpage. Something's wrong with it."

"Oh dear. Is it something you can't fix?" Chase said.

"Not from my end. Can I look at your setup?"

"I'll show you," Mallory said. She abruptly slid out from behind the counter and beckoned Tanner into the kitchen.

What was that about? Chase wondered. Of course, Mallory knew where the computer was, in the office off the kitchen. But she wouldn't know where to find anything on it. She called after them. "Let me know if you need help!" Then she continued whittling down the line of buyers before her, all with their arms full of her wares.

When Mallory emerged a few minutes later, she told Chase that Tanner was trying a few things to fix the website. Chase did a double take at the pink glow on her cheeks. It seemed that Mallory was smitten. She smiled at the thought and kept working.

Tanner reappeared in the salesroom in under ten minutes. "That cat must have unplugged the router. If it's okay with you, I want to look up something. Then I'll be off."

"Wait a sec," Chase said. "I'll go with you."

She should make sure Quincy was still in the office, since she had neglected to mention him to the pair when they headed that way. But she had another idea, too.

TEN

Chase watched Tanner glide through some computer screens she had never seen before. They were not only unfamiliar, they were weird-looking. "What's that?" she asked.

"It's your code. It's what's behind your webpages. I think I need to tweak a couple of things."

She wasn't sure how to state her question. "How are you at . . . getting into things?"

Tanner gave her a questioning glance. "What do you mean? What things?"

Chase sat on the edge of the desk and looked down at Tanner, who was occupying her desk chair. "Have you been following the murder of Ron North?"

FAT CAT TAKES THE CAKE

He nodded with excitement. "The guy you found with your cat? That is totally . . . different."

She thought he'd been about to say it was awesome. It totally was not awesome. Not to her and not to Julie.

"I mean, I heard on the web that he was strangled with a scarf. And it belongs to your friend Julie, right? That's not good."

Chase agreed. "I need to convince the police that she didn't do it."

"How do you know she didn't?"

Good question. Julie had disappeared right after Ron North left the reunion. She could have followed Ron to the parking lot, briefly. She could have gotten her scarf back. But Chase hadn't seen it again—until she encountered it wrapped around Ron's neck. She knew her best friend wasn't a killer. "Ron North had lots of enemies. He was an annoying person and might have been blackmailing people."

"Whoa. That could get him dead."

"Yes, it could."

"So, who all was he blackmailing?"

When Chase didn't answer, he caught on. "You want to find out, right? You want me to hack into his, like, online stuff?"

"Would you know where to find things like that?"

"That's what you meant about getting into things. Private messages and stuff. I might. Give me a few minutes."

Chase left him to it. The thought crossed her mind that he would probably be able to access everything on her computer. But there wasn't much there that she wanted to keep secret. She hoped he wouldn't hack into her bank account and steal all of her cash. Somehow, she couldn't picture Tanner doing that.

Anna raised her eyebrows, questioning Chase as she passed through the kitchen.

"Later," Chase mouthed.

"Is he still here?" Mallory asked when Chase returned to the front of the shop.

"He's doing some extra work for me."

She was able to lose herself in dessert bar sales for two hours without thinking about Tanner and what he might be into. When he poked his head into the salesroom and beckoned her, she followed him to the office. He'd been there much longer than he'd thought he would.

"What did you find?" Not her own passwords, she hoped.

"All kinds of stuff." He was zinging with excitement. "I haven't had this much fun since the release of *Call of the Aura Assassins*." His fingers shook as they hovered over the keyboard for a moment, then steadied as they danced across it. A screen of exchanges came up. "Look at these e-mails."

Chase bent to get a better angle on the screen. One set of messages was from "rnorth83," the other from "bigbyrd." She scanned them. The most interesting e-mails were near the bottom.

bigbyrd: mona sez u followed her again 2day. this is your last warning.

rnorth83: or what?

bigbyrd: i go to the cops

rnorth83: and i release my pictures. i no where you were last nite and it wasnt at home. was it.

"Bigbyrd must be Richard Byrd. It's kind of hard to read that stuff, isn't it? These almost look like text messages rather than e-mails." Chase said.

Tanner blinked. "Why?"

"You don't have to stop and think about what that means?"

"I think it means that North was stalking Byrd's wife or girlfriend. Byrd wants him to stop, but North has some kind of pictures that Byrd doesn't want anyone to see."

So no, the e-mail shorthand was not a puzzle to Tanner, Chase thought. "And North knows something about Byrd being somewhere that he shouldn't have been. I mean North *knew* that."

"Right. He's not threatening anyone now, is he? Byrd, I mean."

"They were threatening each other," Chase said. "I wonder if this was a stalemate. I don't remember hearing about any incriminating photos of Dickie. What's the date of this exchange?"

Tanner scrolled up. "Two weeks ago."

"Oh, recently. So this is fresh stuff. The police need to know about this."

Tanner blanched and his fingers stilled. "No, you can't do that. You can't tell them I hacked in here."

Chase nodded slowly. "Yes, I see that." But she had the knowledge. She should be able to find another way to get the information to the police. After all, she had seen Byrd kissing that woman. Maybe North had pictures of those two.

And maybe Byrd spent some time with that woman when he was supposed to be somewhere else. Like at home. How would she go about ferreting out this stuff?

"Thanks, Tanner. This is a big help."

He got up and stretched. He'd been sitting for over two hours straight and even his young body must have felt stiff. "No problem. Let me know if you need anything else like this. It's fun stuff."

"Can I get you something to drink? To eat?"

He glanced at the time in the corner of the computer monitor. "No, I better go. I'm late."

After he left, she checked whether any pages were open that referenced material she would rather he didn't see. There didn't seem to be, but how easy would it be for Tanner to cover his tracks? He sure knew his way around a computer. Chase wondered if Mike Ramos had known about all of Tanner's talents when he recommended him.

She had a little session with Quincy, giving him his Kitty Patty and a Go Go Ball, then headed for the salesroom through the kitchen.

"Julie called," Anna said. She was up to her elbows in powdered sugar, sprinkling it with flair over a new batch of Hula Bars. It must have been the wintry feel to the weather that was selling the pineapple-coconut concoctions like hotcakes. They tasted like summer. Anna had been baking them all morning to replenish the supply. "She's bringing lunch."

"She's not working today?"

"She said something about having to be in the neighborhood. I'll bet that's her now."

They both heard the back door open and Julie appeared a moment later, laden with Mexican takeout bags.

"Mmm," Chase said, sniffing the tangy aroma of the flavored meat. "Tacos or burritos?"

"Some of each," Julie said, depositing the bags on the center island counter. "I got some for Mallory, too. Inger's not working today, right? That's what Grandma said." Julie sounded fine, but there was worry in her eyes. Her face was tight.

"She had a doctor's appointment this morning," Chase said. "She's coming in later this afternoon."

"Good," Julie said. "I would have picked up something a bit more bland if I'd thought she would be here."

"She's all done with morning sickness, but she still doesn't like to be around spicy food," Anna said. "That's understandable."

Chase remembered what a picky eater Inger had been when she'd stayed in her apartment after her parents kicked her out.

"Anna said you had to be in the area," Chase said, picking up a soft taco and biting off the end. "Mm. Love these." The cheese melted on her tongue, mitigating the spicy beef a tad.

"I'm going to visit Hilda Bjorn again about my pro bono case, right after we eat. It's been crazy at work."

"Oh good," Chase said. "I'd sure like to know what's going on with that. Is a pro bono case confidential?"

"Well, yes. But if I find anything criminal is going on, I'll turn it over to the DA's office."

"Will you know that just from talking to her?" Anna asked.

"Maybe. Maybe not. But I can contact some of my former colleagues there and they can dig if I think they need to."

"It has to be criminal, doesn't it?" Chase said, reaching for another taco. "Offering such a ridiculously low price?"

"They're taking advantage of an old woman." Anna didn't consider herself old, of course.

"They're not the only ones," Julie said. "You'd be amazed at how many seniors get swindled over the phone and the Internet."

"My cousin," Anna said, "gave out her credit card number and her bank account information to someone who called offering her life insurance. She never saw the insurance, or the five thousand dollars the crook took out of her bank account."

"That's awful," Julie said. "Did she tell someone?"

"Yes. She lives in Oregon and the authorities have all the information. I don't think they caught anyone, but the bank says they'll make good on the money. She has no idea how long that will take."

Julie stuffed her burrito wrapper into the now empty bag and rinsed her fingers at the sink. "I'd better get going."

"I wish I could come and hear what Ms. Bjorn says." Chase was picking up the tidbits that had dropped from her tacos.

Julie gave her a stern look. "You know you can't do that."

She did know. Julie had broken so many rules for her, though, that she sometimes lost sight of the boundaries. However, Chase thought she could probably find out the gist of their conversation from the horse's mouth—Hilda Bjorn. Or maybe even from Professor Fear. He was so good about taking care of his neighbor. And, if the rumors were true, he would soon receive a similar offer on his house.

"See you later." Julie smiled as she swept out the back door.

Chase gathered up the last of the debris. "I'll go get Mallory to eat her lunch."

"Let me take a turn up front," Anna said. "I haven't worked the floor today. I don't think there's any kitchen work that needs doing. I may make another batch later."

"You don't need to practice for the Batter Battle?"

"Tonight I will. Bill is going to come here to talk about his suit for the wedding and I'll work on my technique."

Chase decided to catch up on paperwork in the office. The phone on the desk rang before she sat down. She didn't recognize the number. "Yes?"

"Hey, Eddie here. You free for lunch tomorrow?"

Her heart raced at the thought of Eddie Heath. She wished it wouldn't, but it did just the same. "Hi, Eddie. I'm not sure. I usually work here all day."

"You wanna check?"

She didn't want to go to his health bar, she was sure about that. But she needed to talk to someone who knew these people. He knew the principal and Dickie Byrd, of course, and Ron North. But she hadn't found anyone who knew Langton Hail, the funny little guy who wore vests. Maybe she would have lunch with him and pick his brain. "I'll call you back in a couple of minutes."

"I'll be waiting here."

She wondered where "here" was. She checked on the kitchen. Mallory was wolfing down a burrito and said she would be ready to return to work in a couple of minutes.

When she poked her head through the doors into the sales-room, Anna was neatening the shelves.

"Not busy?" Chase asked.

"No, not since the six customers who were here when I came out."

Chase returned to her office and sat in her chair, petted Quincy, and pondered whether she should have lunch again with the delectable Eddie Heath, who was a certifiable health nut and who was not Michael Ramos.

ELEVEN

When Bill came over to keep Anna company that evening after the shop closed, Chase stayed to watch Anna practice. She was becoming more and more invested in Anna winning the contest. For about half a minute she considered mentioning her lunch date tomorrow, but decided against that. She needed counsel from someone, but not from Anna when Bill was there. After all, they were getting very close to their wedding day. How could she bother them with relationship issues now? No, she couldn't.

"Chase," Bill said to her as Anna clattered her measuring cups and spoons onto the counter. "What do you know about Julie and this murder business?"

Anna raised her head quickly, lines forming between her eyebrows.

"Not much. It looks like Ron was strangled with her scarf and the police won't let go of that. I know"—or was pretty sure—"that she never had her scarf again after he took it." Chase opened the cupboard and got out the mixing bowls Anna would need.

"So," Anna said, turning her back to the counter for a moment, "the victim had it. Ron North had the scarf and whoever killed him got it from—what, a pocket or something?"

"I saw him stuff it into his pocket," Chase said. "His hip pocket."

"It could have even fallen out," Bill said, taking a seat on one of the stools. "Anyone could have picked it up."

"Julie told me she went outside to meet Bart Fender." Anna spoke slowly. "In the parking lot. He asked for legal advice." Anna's voice dropped and cracked. "Ron North was there, too. But she's told the police she didn't see either one of them, that she wasn't in the parking lot. She's lying to the police." Anna's fists were clenched, wrinkling her apron.

Chase could tell that Anna was getting more and more distraught by the discussion, so she started asking her questions about her baking procedure for the contest, and they quit talking about Julie.

Julie called later that night, after Anna and Bill left. Chase was upstairs, thinking about getting ready for bed. She grabbed the phone, muting the sitcom she was watching.

"Well, can you tell me anything?" Chase asked, eager

for the details. "Have the police finally admitted you didn't do the crime?"

"Not that I know of."

"They at least know you didn't have that scarf, right?"

"Right. But someone told them that I went out to the parking lot after Ron left. I went out there because Bart Fender wanted to ask me a legal question, one that I'm not qualified to handle. So I followed him out, but came right back in. I saw Ron there, so I suppose I could have gotten the scarf from him then."

"But you didn't! Who on earth said that?"

"I don't think they would have told me if I'd asked. Maybe Bart."

"Did you learn anything today that sheds light on the murder?"

"I think I did, actually. Not from Hilda Bjorn. Not yet. But I've been going through those copied pages you gave me, from Ron's notebook."

"Have you figured out the code?"

"No, not the code. I decided to read the other stuff, his notes for stories he intended to write up."

"It was awfully hard to read his writing," Chase said.

"It was, but I've been working at it for the last hour or so. It looks like he was doing a story on the school board. He thought some money was being misspent. He interviewed the principal and did some background investigating on him. If I'm reading this right, he suspected that Mr. Snelson was misappropriating funds. It doesn't help that Ron's spelling is atrocious. Anyway, he also happened upon the fact that Mr. Snelson, along with a big-time developer, Langton Hail, had petitioned the city for a zoning change. They planned to build a large apartment complex on Hilda Bjorn's block, Ron's notes say."

"So the two of them were in it together? Snelson and Hail?"

"Apparently they planned to buy every house on the block."

"For almost nothing?"

"That's about it. Ron's notes say 'less than half their value'— his words."

Chase needed to get over there and ask Ms. Bjorn's next-door neighbor, Professor Fear, if he had gotten an offer from one of them. "So the short guy, Langton Hail, is on the school board *and* is a developer?"

"Appears that way."

"I wonder if Mr. Snelson is really going to quit his job as principal."

"He's been there forever," Julie said. "I'm sure sorry I took on the pro bono, though. The news is starting to report things about the apartment complex. No names yet, but that there are definitely shady dealings. The people at work are giving me dirty looks, like I'm part of that."

"That's not fair. Can you tell them that you're not involved in the land deal?"

"I've tried. Some of them don't believe me. I'm new there and they don't know me. There's been some innuendo in a newspaper column. I never read it, but one of our secretaries mentioned that to me. And this is without Ron North writing about it. I'll be glad to get all of this over with."

After the call ended, Chase studied her pages of Ron's notebook, reconsidering the coded sections. Principal and developer, doing dirty deeds. Eminently blackmailable.

There—she had it! PRINCE was the principal, so PHOTO was the developer. These were the two who both had amounts by their names. Rather large amounts, in fact. They must have been paying Ron not to print the real estate story. A real estate scam and embezzlement from two prominent school board members. Wow. Was the J there because he was planning to try to blackmail Julie, too?

Ron hadn't gotten any money from BIRD, but Chase would bet that was Dickie Byrd, and that it would only have been a matter of time before he had been forced to hand some cash over to Ron. Julie had seen Snelson hand something to Ron at the reunion, but Hail hadn't paid that night. Sure enough, there was one more entry for Snelson than for Hail. So was he blackmailing Snelson also for the school board funds and not Hail? Did Snelson have twice the motive to murder Ron?

She had figured out the parts in blue ink. She nuzzled Quincy's head with her nose. "I did it, Quince." Except for the J that was lightly penciled into the blackmail section.

It was too late to call Julie back. She turned her attention to the pink entries. What she thought of as the Stalking Section. She was pretty sure that M was Monique and J was Julie. But there was also a D. Whoever that was.

The next morning, Anna was dragging. "Too many late nights for me," she said to Chase as they put out the dessert bars for the day. "I'll be so glad when the Batter Battle is over."

"You will be." Chase gave her a smile. "Because you're going to win it."

Anna sighed. "I sure hope I can at least hold my own

against that nasty Grace Pilsen. I'd like to know what her entry is."

"What good would that do you?"

"Then I'd know if I need to be concerned about losing or not."

"I suppose." Chase was doubtful that would be any help. And it didn't matter, since there was no way to find out what Grace's recipe was.

She waited until midmorning to ask Anna if she thought it would be okay to take lunch out. Her hope was that they would be too busy and she'd have to call Eddie and cancel. No such luck. For once, the doldrums hit the salesroom and stayed all morning.

"Go ahead," Anna said. "I baked some extra last night since I was here, so I can help with sales if they pick up. Are you doing something exciting? Seeing Mike?"

"No, meeting a high school friend."

"It's that Eddie person again, isn't it? The man who doesn't like our products."

"Well, yes. I think he might have some information that would help Julie."

Anna gave her a sideways glance. "That would be good." She suspected there was something more, Chase was sure. That woman had Chase's number, and good instincts.

Chase was able to steer Eddie to a lunch place that was a step up from fast food, but definitely not vegan. She told him she didn't have enough time to go to his own health bar. He was disappointed.

"You know how it is when you own your own business,"

she said. "I can't be away for too long in the middle of the day."

"What days are you closed?"

Uh-oh. She'd laid a trap for herself. "We close on Mondays and Tuesdays, usually."

"I'll have to pick you up one of those days, then, and take you to the Health from the Heath Bar. You'll love it."

Chase gave him what she hoped was an enigmatic smile. That was better than sticking her finger in her mouth with her tongue out.

"We can walk to this place today." Chase headed up the street to the Meet N Eat, which was only a few blocks away.

"It's pretty cold out. You sure you don't want me to drive there?"

Chase paused and took in the clear, crisp sunshine, the dark blue sky, and the merest hint of a breeze. "It's a beautiful day. It would be healthier to walk."

She had him there. Chase had to admit, though, that her cheeks were numb and her eyes watering by the time they reached their destination. Eddie was right. It was cold out.

The warmth of the Meet N Eat felt good; it wrapped around her as soon as she entered. Smells of sizzling beef hung in the air, making her realize that the walk had made her hungry.

As they went in, two men were going out, and one of them was Langton Hail.

After they were out the door, Eddie noticed Chase eyeing them. "Do you know who that was?" he asked. "He seems familiar."

"He's the guy we saw at that vegan restaurant who was drunk. He was at the reunion. He's nobody important." *Unless he's a murderer.* Eddie, she thought, obviously didn't know anything about the man.

Eddie waited until they were seated by the hostess before he began criticizing Chase's choice.

"What kind of a menu is this? Look at all this beef."

"It's a hamburger restaurant," Chase said. "They specialize in beef."

"There are exactly five vegetables on here. And two are breaded and fried."

"I always get lettuce and tomato on my cheeseburger."

Eddie shuddered, but stopped complaining.

Chase studied the menu, thinking she might try something different than her usual cheeseburger with onion rings (presumably one of the unacceptable vegetables). Maybe she'd go with the Chicken Caesar Salad. That might appease Mr. Health Heath a bit.

He ordered the Chicken Caesar Salad, too, the only Caesar on the menu, but no chicken—and no dressing. Just Romaine lettuce, basically, Chase thought.

The hostess brushed by and seated a couple at the table next to them. Chase was horrified to see Mike Ramos. She turned her head aside quickly and tried to keep her face hidden. However, she had to know who he was with, so she snuck a peek. One look at the dark brown shoulder-length hair told Chase this was his cousin, Patrice Youngren. The young woman was a self-styled fortune-teller. She was also a habitual thief. She loved the thrill of lifting things and not getting caught. The trouble was, she often got caught. She had managed, though, to filch a ring off Chase's finger once without Chase noticing until much later. Mike had gotten it back and Patrice had promised not to take anything from Chase again.

"Chase, hi," Patrice said, spotting her and waving with a bright smile. "Good to see you."

Mike, who had been seated with his back to Chase (so that Chase had thought she might get away without being noticed by him), whipped around, started to smile, and spied Eddie. The smile died before it was completely born.

This was too awkward. Mike would think it strange if she didn't introduce Eddie.

"Hi, Mike," Chase said. "This is Eddie Heath. He owns a health bar here in Minneapolis." Maybe he'd think this was a business lunch and they were discussing their prospective shops. Or maybe it wouldn't be such a bad thing for him to be a bit jealous.

The guys and Patrice said hi and that seemed to be the end of it, except for Mike's deep scowl directed at Chase.

Eddie tried to make small talk while they waited for their food to arrive. "You know, funniest thing. I drive by the high school on my way to work and there was a car still there the morning after the reunion. I think we missed part of the party."

"You think some people stayed there all night?"

"Probably too drunk to drive home. There was someone in the car, sleeping it off. Hard liquor is toxic to your body, you know."

Chase didn't think a glass of liquor was exactly "toxic," but she didn't feel like arguing with the guy.

He asked how the Bar None was doing. "Do people buy all those things made with sugar and flour?"

"The shop is going great guns," Chase said. "My partner, Anna, is a little frantic with all she has going on right now."

Eddie raised his eyebrows in question.

"First of all, she's getting married Christmas Eve."

"My Health from the Heath Bar does a terrific reception buffet." He paused. "But I suppose your place will supply the catering."

Chase nodded. "She's also entered in the Minny Batter Battle. She'd like very much to win. A woman named Grace Pilsen is a rival of Anna's and has been taunting her unmercifully."

"Who is she?"

"She owns a bakery called The Pilsener."

Eddie guffawed. "Really? It's a bakery, not a bar?"

"Really. Anna would love to get hold of Grace's recipe so she would know what she has to beat."

"That would probably help her out a lot, wouldn't it?"

"I think so. I'm not into stealing recipes, though, and neither is she."

Their food arrived and Chase noticed, out of the corner of her eye, a rapt expression on Patrice's face. Mike's posture was stiff and unnatural. His face was buried in his menu. She could almost feel the frost emanating from him.

TWELVE

As soon as Chase got to the Bar None, Anna hurried over. "Good, you're back. Are you doing anything tonight?"

Chase took off her coat and scarf and hung them on a hook by the rear door. "Nothing special." She had thought she would inspect the state of their inventory and maybe go over the financials for the shop.

"I've just talked to Julie. She's feeling pretty low. We need to cheer her up."

"Okay. I'm all for that. What do you have in mind?"

"*Holmes Sweet Holmes* is playing tonight at the Orpheum. Julie's talked about it and I think it would do her good to get her mind off everything."

"Don't you want to practice for the Batter Battle tonight?"

"I'm getting sick of it, to tell you the truth. I could use a night off. Then I'll hit it fresh on Friday."

"And win the contest next Saturday!" Chase had no desire to do the books tonight. They'd be there tomorrow.

"One hopes."

Chase went to the office to try to do a little work on ordering items for the shop. That was something she had to keep up with. If they ran out of baking supplies, they were out of product to sell. They could run to the local grocer for a few things, but she needed to stay on top of the major items. She completed most of her ordering, but didn't know if they needed more eggs or not. Those were ordered separately from a local farmer. So she went into the kitchen to count them.

Mallory stuck her head into the kitchen, spotted Chase, then came over close to her. "Ms. Oliver? Someone is here to see you." Her voice was quiet.

"Who is it?"

"She didn't tell me. She said she has something for you."

Chase gave Anna a shrug, closed the refrigerator, and went to see who it was. Patrice, Mike's cousin, stood by the glass case, her back to Chase, gazing out the front windows to the shops across the street. She turned when she heard Chase and Mallory come in.

"Hi, Patrice," Chase said. "Mallory says you have something for me?"

"Is there somewhere private we can talk?"

Now Chase was truly puzzled. She ushered Patrice through the kitchen, to the office. Quincy, showing no favorites, twined around first Chase's legs, then Patrice's after Chase closed the door. Anna had given them a quick glance, no doubt wondering what was going on.

"Hello, you handsome fellow." Patrice stooped to pet Quincy and his purr motor started on high.

"What is it you have, Patrice?"

She looked around the room.

"Would you like to sit down?"

"No, I won't be long. I came to give you this, but please don't tell anyone where you got it from." She opened her small purse and pulled out a folded paper. After a moment's hesitation, she thrust it at Chase.

"I heard you talking at lunch," she said. "I thought you would like to have this."

Chase was getting a bad feeling about whatever it was she held. She slowly unfolded the paper. At the top of the sheet, in all caps, it said "BANANA RICE WONDER CAKE." Scanning down, it seemed to be a cake recipe, made with rice flour. "What is this?"

"You said Anna would like to see Grace Pilsen's recipe."

Chase's mouth dropped open. "You . . . stole Grace's recipe?"

"You said Anna needed to see it."

"I don't think I said she *needed* to see it."

"It sounded like you said that."

Patrice had been listening in on her and Eddie. Chase had known that at the time, but hadn't foreseen the consequences. After all, Patrice got a kick out of stealing things.

Chase tapped on the paper, trying to decide what to do.

She had already seen it, so she couldn't pretend she hadn't. "Is this the only copy? Does Grace have another one?"

Patrice nodded. "I copied it and put it right where I found it."

The woman was a skillful thief, Chase had to admit. "And no one saw you do it?"

"Of course not."

"How did you get this?"

"I don't think I can to tell you that. It's my secret."

Chase didn't want to go into the business of stealing recipes, but was curious how Patrice had gone about it. However, she wasn't going to find out.

"This is going to help you out, isn't it? I wanted to make up for taking your ring at the fair."

"Yes. Well, I guess this will do it. We're completely even now. You don't need to steal any more things for me, Patrice." She meant well, Chase thought. Didn't she?

After Patrice left, Chase stayed in her office, ostensibly finishing up her work, but really dithering about what to do with the recipe. On the one hand, she thought this would be an easy one to beat. The ingredients wouldn't go together well. Rice flour needed a stronger flavor than banana to make a delectable dessert. The cake recipe wasn't likely to wow the judges. So not showing it to Anna shouldn't change a thing. On the other hand, Anna seemed so very nervous about competing with Grace that it might make her feel better knowing Grace's entry wasn't a winner. But, if Chase had a third hand, there was something else to consider. Was this actually Grace's recipe? Even if it belonged to her, was it the one she was using for the Batter Battle?

Since Chase had no idea where or how Patrice had gotten it, she couldn't be sure it was the real thing. She wouldn't show it to Anna. Tucking it into the pocket of the smock she hadn't taken off, she felt good about that decision. It sounded busy out front, so she went to help out until closing time.

It would be fun going to the show tonight with Anna and Julie.

THIRTEEN

The show was perfect, both hilarious and dramatic, with snappy songs that Chase was sure would rattle around inside her head for days. In fact, as they were leaving the show, Chase realized she had forgotten about the whole Ron-North-murdered, Julie-Larson-suspected mess. Maybe Julie had, too.

"You know, that developer, Langton Hail, had an excellent motive to want Ron North dead," Julie said, climbing into the backseat of Anna's Volvo.

Chase, already belted in the front seat, realized that Julie hadn't forgotten about a thing. She twisted around to talk to Julie. "Have you been thinking about this all during the show?"

"No. Well, a little bit. Detective Olson has to talk to me at the station again tomorrow."

Chase turned to the front and tried not to let her dismay show.

"But developing property," Julie went on, "buying cheap and making money on it, is Hail's livelihood. He would have a lot to lose if Ron's story cast him in a bad light. It might have made someone investigate what he's doing. Even if it only shut him down for a while, it would hurt."

"And," Chase said, turning halfway around again as Anna started the car, "it looks like Hail was paying blackmail money to Ron. If so, he knows that what he's doing is wrong."

Anna cranked the heater up all the way. Chase stuck her hands next to the vent. She hadn't been able to find her good gloves and hadn't wanted to wear her disreputable everyday ones with the holes to the theater.

"You know, Eddie said that someone might have slept in his car all night after the reunion."

"Someone who got awfully drunk, you mean," Julie said.

"Yes, maybe he stayed there to sleep it off instead of driving."

"It was cold that night," Anna said.

"So," Julie said, "this person might have spent part of the night killing Ron North, then slept in his car for a bit. What exactly did Eddie see?"

"You're seeing a lot of Eddie," Anna said to Chase.

Chase ignored Anna. "He saw a car and someone was in it."

"That doesn't mean anything, then, does it?" Julie said.

"Someone could have killed Ron and he could have been too drunk to move after that. It's a wonder he didn't freeze to death."

"God," Anna said, "protects fools and drunks."

"And if you're both," Chase added, "you're doubly blessed, aren't you?"

Chase hated the fact that Olson was continuing to badger Julie. She would call him first thing in the morning to tell him to take a closer look at who might have been in the car the morning after the reunion.

When she got home from the theater it was late and she had to open the shop in the morning.

The treat giver started to go into her bedroom. However, the cat ran ahead of her and started howling. When she noticed, he ran into the kitchen. That was when she realized that he hadn't had a single treat today, only din dins. After the treat was warmed and put into his dish, he let her know what a transgression this was by turning his back, gulping down the treat, then, after a whisker cleanse, jumping onto the couch for the night.

"Oh, come on, you're not so mad that you're going to sleep on the couch, are you?" Chase said, her hands on her hips as she regarded the indignant cat. "I might as well have a husband."

Once again, she headed for the bedroom. She always left the door open, so she figured Quincy would be in sooner or later, to sleep on the bed, which was made much cozier than the couch by having a human in it. As she began to drowse, she felt his warm body snuggle up to her back. She fell asleep to the sound of deep, throaty purring. The moment before she lost consciousness, she thought that maybe a cat would be better than ever having a husband. Especially one who stood you up to class reunions.

First thing in the morning, before she could call the police station, Mike rang her.

"It's Friday," he said.

"Yes, it is."

"Hey, you're not still mad, are you? I'd like to take you to dinner tonight. There's a new place on the other side of campus. Small, Italian. One of my patient's owners likes it, and she's Italian, so it should be good."

Was she to ignore the fact that he was shooting daggers at her yesterday? Or was he taking her to dinner to make it up to her?

"Sure," she said. "That sounds nice."

"You're not busy with that other guy?"

Chase huffed into the phone. "He's a *business* associate. It was a *business* meeting." Sort of. If she said it enough times, maybe it would be true. Maybe she would forget that tingle she got when Eddie touched her. "What time tonight?"

After they settled the details and hung up on good terms— as far as Chase could tell—she dialed Detective Niles Olson.

His answer was abrupt. That either meant he was very busy solving the murder, or he recognized her number and wasn't looking forward to speaking with her. "Olson here," he barked.

"Detective, I've come into some information—"

"What else is new?" Did he have to sound so weary?

"I wasn't questioning anyone, I just learned that a car was in the parking lot of Hammond High Sunday morning."

"You saw a car there? Whose was it?"

"No, Eddie Heath saw it. I don't know whose it was. Probably the killer's, don't you think?"

"There's no reason to think that, because a car was left in the parking lot, it belongs to a killer. Some heavy drinking was going on and someone probably had the good sense to leave a car there and get a ride." There was a pause. Was that a good sign? "The car wasn't there when we processed the scene, so the driver must have left early. Hail and Snelson both said they spent the night together at Snelson's house. Hail was too drunk to drive. Snelson's wife even backed him up. I'll find out if Langton left his car there, but this might not mean anything, Chase."

It worked so much better when he was calling her "Chase" and not "Ms. Oliver."

"There might have been someone in the car," she said. *Depending on how much she trusted what Eddie thought he saw.* "You're welcome."

"Yeah, thanks. But"—his voice grew stern—"do not do any digging into this. We'll figure out whose car it was."

"I told you, I wasn't digging. If I hear anything else I should tell you, right?"

"Yes, but don't do anything about it. Tell me and no one else. And stay away from Snelson and Hail. I'm sure you know what I'm talking about."

She did. One of them could be a killer. They had alibied

each other, but both could be lying. If so, where were they that night? Whose car was in the parking lot? She wasn't going to investigate, not exactly, not officially, but she sure was going to keep her ears open.

As she dressed, she glanced out the window. Lovely, soft flakes of snow were falling. It lifted her spirits when the flakes of perfect crystals floated past her window. She hummed "My Favorite Things" from *The Sound of Music* on her way downstairs.

Both Inger and Mallory were working the front today, so she hung out in the kitchen with Anna, helping put together some treats. Anna had hit upon a wonderful bakeless Chocolate Peanut Butter Bar that could be made quickly and easily. Of course, nothing could exactly be easy with Anna in the picture. So she and Anna were piping frosting in the shapes of stars, Christmas trees, and holly wreaths on each piece in red and green frosting.

When Inger came in for her lunch break, she was enchanted with their efforts. "How soon can we start selling those? We won't be able to keep them in the shop. Everyone will love them."

"Try it," Anna said, holding out a star-decorated bar.

Inger bit into it. "I've died and gone to heaven."

Chase wasn't crazy about peanut butter and chocolate together, but she knew a whole lot of people were. This was a good idea.

She went to cover for Inger while she ate lunch. Soon after she entered the salesroom, Bart Fender burst into the shop. Of course, he probably burst into any room he entered. He was a very physical person. Short, but powerfully built. He wore a stocking cap on his bald head, protecting it against the cold.

"Bart," Chase said. "How nice that you've dropped in." She hadn't seen him in years until the reunion. He hadn't changed much, except for piling on some more muscles and losing all his hair. He'd been an athlete then and remained one today as the high school wrestling coach.

"Thought I'd look the place over. What do you have here?"

"Lots of different flavored dessert bars. Do you have a favorite?"

He took off his gloves and rubbed his chin. "I'm not much on chocolate. Used to be, but sweets don't taste that sweet anymore. I don't know what it is. Maybe the situation with Dillon."

"What do you know? Any changes?"

"No, and there aren't going to be." He frowned. "Her family . . . they drive me crazy. They won't admit . . . Oh, enough about that. Do you have something that's super sweet?" He was a couple of inches shorter than Chase, but stood with a wide stance and took up nearly the whole aisle between the tables of products.

She pointed out the Raspberry Chiffon Bars. "These are pretty sweet, and there's the delicious raspberry taste."

His eyes lit up. "I like raspberry. I'll try a couple of those. Maybe I could taste them better." He cocked his elbow back to extract his wallet from his jeans pocket. Unfortunately, his elbow connected with a pile of stacked dessert boxes and they tumbled to the floor. The floor was tracked with melting, rather slushy snow.

Bart turned an alarming shade of red. Not just his face,

but his whole head. It wasn't embarrassment, more like anger at something. Himself? The easily dislodged boxes? His lips curled into a snarl and invectives streamed from between his clenched teeth.

"It's okay, Bart." Chase hoped he couldn't tell how scared she was. He was a volcano about to erupt. His reaction seemed entirely out of proportion. "We'll take these and repackage the goodies that got wet. The dessert bars are probably fine."

Mallory was already swooping up the fallen wares and whisking them into the kitchen. She cringed, as frightened of the man as Chase felt.

Chase touched his arm. One of his fists unclenched, then the other. "No big deal, Bart. Really. Why don't you take these two on trial? If you like them, come back and buy some more." She slid the bars into a bag and held it out to him.

He swiped it with a hammy fist. He gave a grimace that was probably supposed to be a sheepish grin, and stalked out.

Chase deflated a bit when the door closed. Then she squared her shoulders and continued waiting on the steady stream of customers. The shop was so crowded, most of them hadn't noticed a thing.

FOURTEEN

Chase thought about Bart Fender as she waited on other customers. If he couldn't taste sweet things, he probably wouldn't be back. Probably a good thing since he barely fit into the store. In fact, she wondered if all that bulk was natural. It was possible he took performance-enhancing drugs. But he came into contact with young high school athletes daily. She hoped his bad habit—if that was the cause of his massive body—wasn't rubbing off onto his students. She was so glad she wasn't going to high school now! Back then, as far as she knew, the principal hadn't been raking money from the school system and she was sure the coaches weren't taking illegal drugs.

As she was counting change for one of the regulars, Mrs.

Cray, she saw Mr. Snelson walk past on the sidewalk. She must have stared at him, because Mrs. Cray turned around to see what was getting Chase's attention.

"Oh, Mr. Snelson," she said. "He's quite a character."

"You know him?" Chase asked.

"Why, yes. I clean the high school, you know."

"No, I didn't. How long have you been doing that?" The last Chase knew, Mrs. Cray was cleaning offices at the university.

"I started this year. Mrs. Snelson got me the job. She works in the office at the U, you know."

Chase didn't know that either, but was more interested in what Mrs. Cray knew about the principal. She would not have to ask, though. Mrs. Cray was the chatty sort.

"It was kind of strange last weekend. There was that big thing, you know. The reunion."

Chase nodded. She did know that.

"So they asked me to clean on Sunday instead of Saturday, my regular day. There's one thing I don't like about that man."

She paused for effect while Chase waited for her to go on. "He told me on Sunday that he can't stand teenagers. Do you believe that? I mean, I never heard such a thing. He can't stand teenagers? Why does he have that job? That's what I'd like to know."

Aha, thought Chase. After all of those years confronting the pupils, dealing with truants and kids who didn't care if they never finished school, or athletes who assumed the school owed them something, it sounded like he'd had enough. That was, no doubt, why he was getting into real estate.

That evening, Mike rang the bell at the rear door before the tidying-up in the kitchen was completed.

"Oh, there's Mike, Anna," Chase said. "He's early."

Anna grinned. "I'm glad you're back with him. There's something about that other—" She stopped short as Mike strolled in.

"Ready?" he asked.

"I can be in two minutes. Have a seat and a leftover Lemon Chiffon Bar."

Mike hoisted himself onto a stool and Anna set the goodie on a paper towel in front of him. She was asking him if he'd like lemonade with that as Chase ran up the stairs to pass a brush through her hair, wriggle into a clean pair of jeans, slip on a fresh sweater, and swish some mouthwash. She found herself humming "Tonight" from *West Side Story* and realized she was truly happy she wouldn't be eating vegan food tonight, to say nothing of being with Mike.

The Italian food at Mike's discovered restaurant was perfect. Or maybe it was so delicious because of her recent experiences with Eddie. The man himself was delectable, but eating with him was not.

Mike didn't seem inclined to talk about Eddie, which relieved Chase.

"You'll never guess who came into the clinic today," he said.

The question didn't call for an answer, which was good, because Chase's mouth was full of lasagna. Good beefy, cheesy, noodle-y lasagna.

"Mrs. Snelson. She said her husband's the principal of Hammond High."

Chase finished her bite of goodness. "Is she a new customer for you?"

"Yes, her dog is a new patient. I don't think she's had him for very long. Was he the principal when you went there?"

"Yes. He was at the . . . Yes, he's been there forever." She stopped talking, not wanting to mention the sore subject of the reunion.

"She mentioned that. She said he's having trouble adjusting to the dog."

Mike warmed her heart with his smile and topped off her wineglass with the Chianti Reserva he had selected. Its full-bodied taste was perfect with the robust Italian flavors. The candle on the table flickered and danced, helping create an intimate space where only the two of them and the table of delicious food existed.

"What does that mean? Have they never had a dog before? I don't think they ever had children." She forked another piece of lasagna. Yum.

Mike swirled some of his spaghetti carbonara, but didn't take a bite. "Sounded like he might be allergic. She hasn't had him long. He's a tiny lap dog, teacup Chihuahua."

"Is he cute?"

Mike shrugged and took his bite. After a bit he said, "I prefer more natural breeds. This one is neurotic."

Chase thought a lot of Chihuahuas were neurotic. "Can you be allergic to such a tiny dog?"

"Sure. Size doesn't matter. What got me, though, was what she was saying to me, as a perfect stranger. She brought up your reunion and how awful the murder was. Then she repeated, several times, that her husband and a business colleague were together at her house all night, so they couldn't possibly have known anything about the killing."

"Why would she talk about that with you?"

"The more she went on, the more I thought she was trying to convince me. And, I should add, the more I thought she was lying. Why she would need to tell me this, I don't know."

"Maybe," Chase said, "she was rehearsing her story for the police."

FIFTEEN

"Detective Olson, please." Chase had called the station Saturday morning after the homicide detective didn't answer his cell phone. She heard her back door opening. A minute later Anna called up the stairs that she was here. Chase ran to the top of the stairs and motioned to her that she was on the phone. Anna nodded and proceeded into the kitchen. Quincy slipped down the stairs. She would have to make sure he got into the office before they opened for business.

"Yes?"

She tried to detect his mood from that single word. He didn't seem angry or abrupt this time. The receptionist probably told him who was calling, so that must have meant she wasn't on his bad side at the moment.

"I talked with my friend Dr. Ramos last night. He told me that Mrs. Snelson, who owns a little tiny dog, was talking to him about her husband being with Langton Hail all night after the reunion."

"Yes, that's also what she told us."

"Well, don't you think that's odd?"

"It's odd that a married couple has a friend over? No, I don't think so. Why would you?"

"But all night? It's not something people go around saying. She's, well, she's protesting too much. Know what I mean?"

"Yes, I've read Shakespeare." He was silent for a moment. She heard Anna humming the chorus of "Dancing Through Life" from *Wicked* in the kitchen as she waltzed, Chase was sure, from counter to stove to refrigerator.

"Okay, Chase," Niles Olson said. "I agree it's a strange thing to talk about. How well does she know Dr. Ramos?"

"Not at all. She's a brand-new customer at his clinic."

"I'll make a note. Thanks for calling."

That was a tiny bit of progress, Chase thought. There must be a guilty secret there, some fire under the smoke. It made some sense that, if Hail were too drunk to drive, he might go home with Snelson, since he lived close to the school. She needed to think this through. Later.

Right now, she needed to get to work. It was Saturday, with only a week and a half to go before Christmas. The closer the holidays got, the more people craved sweets.

The pudgy tabby was enjoying himself immensely. He didn't usually get this much time in the kitchen in the morning.

*Normally, his feeder person let him downstairs, then
herded him into the office straightaway. While she lingered
upstairs on the phone, though, the older woman was content to let him wander the room, trolling for tidbits that
hadn't been mopped up the night before. If they were there,
he couldn't find them. Too soon, the feeding woman came
downstairs and shut him into the office. He checked to make
sure the paper he'd hidden was still under the desk. This
room was never cleaned nearly as thoroughly as the kitchen.
Otherwise, it wouldn't still be sitting there, right where he
had stuffed it.*

"How was your date last night?" Anna asked, as soon
as Chase took care of corralling Quincy and came to help
get the day started.

"Very nice."

"I can tell from your smile." Anna set up a racket getting out the metal baking pans.

Chase cocked her head, recalling part of her conversation with Mike. "He said that Mrs. Snelson is one of his
new customers."

"That's our principal's wife? Our principal who wants
to do real estate scams?"

"Yes, indeed. And he was most likely being blackmailed
for that. Even so, maybe he didn't kill Ron North. He and
the little guy he was with spent the night at Snelson's house.
What about Dickie Byrd? He might be a better suspect. I
doubt he'll get elected. If even *I* have seen him with another
woman, I'll bet a lot of other people have, too. In fact, Ron

North was probably planning on blackmailing him." She was recalling the "BIRD" on the blackmail book. It didn't have a dollar amount next to it, but surely it would have if Ron had lived longer.

Mallory and Inger arrived at the same time, bringing a burst of frigid air in with them from the parking lot.

Chase sniffed the air. It smelled moist, like it might snow soon.

"You're both early," Anna said.

"It's been so crazy," Inger said, "I thought I would get a head start."

"Here are the trays of dessert bars for the case." Anna pulled some from the refrigerator and Mallory and Inger both started carrying them to the front.

The morning wore on with a few deliveries and lots of customers. After Chase and Anna got several batches of bars baked, filling the shop with the aromas of cinnamon, lemon, and cherry—which blended surprisingly well— Chase decided to get started on payroll. Monday was the fifteenth and she would pay Mallory and Inger then.

She greeted Quincy with a head rub as he jumped up onto the desk, settling beside her keyboard. She toiled over the tax tables and state forms for an hour, then stood, ready for lunch. Quincy jumped down and dislodged a business card he'd been lying on top of.

"What's this?" Chase bent down to pick it up. "Vita Life for a Vital Life," she read, puzzling over it. Then she turned the card over and saw a name and room number. She remembered it now. This was the card Bart Fender had given to Julie at the reunion. Julie had handed it to Chase and Chase had ended up taking it home. Where had it been until today, a week later?

"Quincy Wincy, did you hide this somewhere? You naughty boy." He was developing a habit of secreting away what must be treasures to him. Maybe he was part dog. Or squirrel.

Bart had told Julie that Dillon would like visitors, but the women who had been talking about her said she was in a coma. Chase remembered Dillon as a volleyball player, clean cut and always bouncy. The women said she had attempted suicide. That didn't square with the cheerful pony-tailed blonde whom Chase remembered. Maybe she and Julie should look in on her and at least find out what was going on. Bart had said something enigmatic about her parents in the shop, too. This was a small mystery, and Chase liked to solve mysteries. She would call Julie tonight and propose they visit on Monday after Julie got home from work.

When Chase went out front so Inger could have lunch, she saw a few lazy flakes circling toward the pavement outside. She hadn't checked a weather report for days, but Mallory assured her that several inches were expected. Chase had filled a watering can in the kitchen and bent to water the poinsettias. Their leaves had started to curl slightly, so they should welcome a drink. She hoped they would stay pretty until Christmas.

"If it starts accumulating, we'll send you home," Chase said, looking out the windows again. "You and Inger. There's no reason for you to have to battle the roads before they're plowed."

Mallory gave her a grateful smile. She had been smiling at the customers more, but Chase thought she forgot about it sometimes, especially when she was rushed and got harried.

A woman in a bright red cloth coat came in and stomped the flakes off her shiny black boots. Her nose and cheeks were almost as red as her coat. Black curly hair framed her round face. After she'd perused the goods in the case and picked out a mix of Lemon and Peanut Butter Fudge Bars, she struck up a conversation with Mallory, who had greeted the woman with a friendly smile that had been returned. Chase nodded to herself when she saw that.

"I'm so glad I found this place. We're entertaining tonight and Van wanted a nice dessert."

"How did you hear about us?" Mallory asked.

Chase was listening in, curious about the mention of "Van." Was she the principal's wife? This woman was the only customer in the store at the moment, so Chase helped bag her choices.

"I found you online," she said. "I searched for desserts and your webpage popped up. It's so attractive and the pictures look delicious."

"I'll have to let our web designer know," Chase said. She would also let Anna know that the efforts she'd been against were paying off.

Anna hurried into the salesroom with some filled boxes to restock the dwindling supplies on the round tables.

"My husband wants to make a good impression tonight. It's for a job."

Chase snuck a peek at her credit card when she handed it over the counter to Mallory. Sure enough, her last name was Snelson. "Are you related to Van Snelson?" Chase asked.

She nodded, beaming with a proud smile.

"He was my principal at Hammond High," Chase said. "I saw him at the reunion last weekend. Were you there?"

"No, no, I didn't go. He said he would be busy talking to important people." She frowned to emphasize how important those people were.

"He spent a lot of time with Mr. Hail, the real estate developer."

"Yes, yes." She brightened. "Van is going into real estate. Langton Hail has been advising him. Langton knows a lot about it. In fact, they spent the rest of the night together and Van didn't come home until the next morning."

Hm, that wasn't exactly the story she had told the detective. "Is he going to resign as principal?" Chase asked.

"Oh my." The woman's hand flew to her cherry-red cheek. "That's not . . . I'm not . . . He hasn't announced anything yet."

Anna gave Mrs. Snelson a curious glance, then retreated to the kitchen.

"Don't worry," Chase said. "I won't tell anyone." *Except Detective Olson.*

Mrs. Snelson signed the bill and took the bag Mallory handed to her. "These will be perfect. They'll love them. I'll be buying more soon." She left with a cheery wave, her faux pas forgotten.

The snow was coming down thicker and the wind was picking up, swirling the flakes in mad, intricate, dizzying patterns.

Chase wished she could see a pattern that led to the real killer of Ron North.

SIXTEEN

In the next hour, so much snow fell that the street blended with the sidewalk, the curbs lost beneath the fluff. Chase and Anna sent Mallory and Inger home while the roads were still passable.

Chase flipped the sign on the front door to "Closed" and went into the kitchen. Inger was in the act of closing the outside door and Chase shivered from the gust that had come into the warm kitchen. "Anna," she said, "you'd better go home, too."

"Let me finish getting this—"

"No, let me finish. You need to get. Come here."

Chase motioned her to the back door. Anna put down the flour bin she'd been about to shelve. Chase shoved the door open, moving a drift about five inches high. The wind was picking up, the snow was falling faster, and the parking lot, as well as the cars, held two to four inches.

"Pretty, isn't it?" Anna said. "You're right. This is going to amount to something." She abandoned the cleaning-up, wrapped herself in her winter clothes, and scooted out the door.

"Call me when you get home," Chase shouted to her departing back. Anna was a careful driver, but you never knew when someone else was going to careen into you and send your car spinning.

"I will!" Anna waved as she swiped the snow off her windshield with her gloved hand. She slipped into the driver's seat, started the engine and the heater, and got out again. Chase watched her clear the back and side windows, then get inside again and drive away.

Chase consulted the weather on her phone. The app predicted six to eight inches. She had been right to send everyone home. She wandered into the front of the store to watch the snow fall. The lights were out inside her shop and, with the snow muffling the sounds from the street, she felt like she was in a cocoon. Quincy settled on top of the glass case, still warm from the lights beneath the glass that had been switched off a short time ago. It was rare for him to be permitted into this part of the shop and he was taking full advantage.

An elderly man passed by, wading through the deepening snow with difficulty. Chase ran to the storage closet and got out the shovel, then pulled on her coat and hat. She wrapped her scarf around her neck and patted her pockets. No gloves. Where were they? They'd been missing for a couple of days now. She dug her old gloves out of her desk drawer, but decided not to use them. They were so full of holes, they would be useless for keeping her hands warm.

When she came in from clearing the sidewalk, she felt virtuous—and cold. Her cheeks were stiff. She made a cup of steaming hot chocolate in the kitchen, as much to thaw her icy hands as to warm her insides.

Maybe everyone was being sent home early. She called Julie on the off chance that she wasn't still at work. She wanted Julie to go with her on Monday to pay a visit to Dillon. If she wanted to go. Maybe Julie would think visiting Dillon in the hospital was a crazy idea. She didn't answer. Probably still slaving away at her desk. Julie was too conscientious for her own good. Maybe, when she'd been at the firm longer, and when she didn't have to worry about being a murder suspect, she would work normal hours.

Two hours later, Chase had made it upstairs and was snuggled with Quincy, watching the snow build up in the lower corners of the window panes in her balcony doors.

"This is exactly like a Christmas card, isn't it, Quincy?"

He turned his amber eyes on her and blinked.

"You agree, don't you?"

Traffic had slowed to an occasional vehicle passing by every five or ten minutes. Those without snow tires slid to a slow stop at the corner. All the drivers on the street seemed to have experience with winter conditions. No one slammed on brakes or fishtailed. The scene was as peaceful as a Christmas card, indeed.

Chase's ringing phone brought her out of her reverie.

"Julie? Are you just getting out?"

Julie breathed heavily into her phone. "Yes. Finally. Jay called Gerrold and he got me out."

Chase shot up from her chair. "What? Out of where?"

"Wait a sec. I have to help Jay scrape his windows."

Chase heard sounds of cars and wind through the tiny speaker. Julie was outside. "Call me right back."

When Julie called, half an hour later, she said she was at home. "I've never been happier to get home."

"What happened? What's been going on?" Chase had fretted the entire thirty minutes.

"I got a call at work as this snow was starting. Detective Olson told me to come to the station."

"In this weather?"

"He doesn't pay attention to weather, apparently." Julie didn't sound at all like herself. Her voice was tight and strangled.

"Go on." Chase couldn't imagine him being deterred by a simple snowstorm.

"He told me I'm being charged with homicide." She sobbed on the last word.

Chase gasped. "Ron North?"

"Who else? I wouldn't say anything to him. I called Jay right away. He had Gerrold Gustafson come by. He had some car trouble, but took a cab and got there in time for my bail hearing. Gerrold got my bail lowered and they released me."

"Thank goodness! They really think you strangled him in the park?"

"No. He wasn't killed there. They think he was killed in the high school parking lot, then dumped under the bush where you found him."

"But why would they zero in on you? Just because it was your scarf?"

"And because I followed Bart out to the parking lot from the reunion." There was a pause. "And because I told them I wasn't out there at first."

"Someone else saw you out there?"

"Only Ron North and Bart Fender. They were arguing about something when I got there."

"So Bart can tell them you didn't kill him!"

"Apparently not. The detective says Bart says he left while I was still out there."

"Where does he say he went?"

"I have no idea. I didn't notice when he left. I spoke five sentences to Bart, then Ron wouldn't leave me alone. I was so spitting mad at him. I told them before that I hadn't seen Ron there, either."

Julie paused again. Was there even more evidence against her?

"And one more thing. I let slip something about the notebook."

"How did you do that?" Chase's heart plummeted. She knew they should have told the detective they had copies.

"I suggested he consider all the stalking victims, not just me. I told him there was a code for the book, so he thinks I'm withholding evidence. He wouldn't believe that we figured out the code. He thinks I have more evidence somewhere. My hearing is next Friday. Gerrold managed to put it off until then by insisting on a judge who is out of town right now. That's when I'll plead not guilty. I'm so glad I don't have to sit in jail until then."

"Friday. This is Saturday. We have five whole days to find out who killed Ron North."

Chase nearly hung up before she remembered why she had called Julie in the first place. Finding Ron North's killer seemed more urgent, but visiting poor Dillon was a good deed she felt she should do. If she wasn't actually in a coma, she would appreciate a report on the reunion. Julie agreed.

"Let's go after I get off work on Monday. I'm going to have to go in Sunday to do all the stuff I was supposed to be catching up on today."

"I'll get some flowers and a card, since I'm not working Monday," Chase offered.

"Deal. I'll pick you up on my way."

"We probably shouldn't mention the murder unless she's already heard about it."

Chase couldn't sit still after the call. Julie had actually been charged with the crime! She wished she had asked Julie whether or not she was going to call Anna. Anna had to be told. Chase waited ten minutes, checking the clock every fifteen to twenty seconds, then called Anna.

"I just got off the phone with her," Anna said. "This can't be happening. It really can't. Julie did not kill that man. Why would they think that?"

Chase had no desire to go into the particulars on the phone. "Julie didn't tell you?"

"Not really. She only said that her scarf was there but I knew that already."

"He was strangled with it. But Ron took it from her earlier."

"There you go. She didn't do it."

Chase agreed, but would that be enough for a judge? Chase doubted it. "There's something else. The detective thinks Julie has evidence she's withholding from him. I neglected to tell anyone we made copies of Ron's notebook and have been trying to decipher his codes. We do think we've decoded some of it, but we don't have anything more than the notebook itself."

"That doesn't seem too awful. I would have made copies."

Chase could have kissed her if they hadn't been on the phone. Even through her cell phone, though, she could hear the shakiness in Anna's voice and could imagine the concern in her bright blue eyes.

After she hung up, she felt like she was jumping out of her prickly skin. She couldn't stay this way until Julie's hearing. She gazed out at the roads. A snowplow rumbled by, scooping the snow to one side and half burying any hapless cars parked at the curbs. She felt like she had to move, had to get out of her apartment. It was so odd to have the shop closed on a Saturday afternoon. If the weather were better, she would take Quincy out for some leash training. He wouldn't appreciate getting his paws soaked, though. She decided instead to take herself for a walk to try to calm her nerves.

She had everything on—boots, scarf, coat, her old gloves— had gone down the stairs, and was opening the door when her cell phone rang. She stepped back inside to answer it.

"Is everything all right over there?" Mike asked.

"Yes. We closed the shop because I was afraid no one could get home if we stayed open until six."

"You have power? I lost mine at the clinic."

She poked her head into the kitchen. The clock lights glowed on the stove and microwave, one showing four thirty-five, the other showing four thirty-eight. She and Anna never managed to get all the clocks in sync. "We're okay here."

"Can I bring some things over? My power has been out all day and I need to keep the insulin refrigerated overnight. My neighbor says power is out at the condo, too. I'm boarding two diabetic cats at the clinic this weekend. It's not supposed to get extremely cold, so I think the cats will be all right. The insulin will be okay for a short time, but I don't want it to get too warm or too cold. I loaned my generator to a friend for the weekend. Bad timing."

"Sure." She knew those tiny vials wouldn't take up much room. "When are you coming?"

"I've canceled everyone but the next appointment, so in about an hour?"

That would be plenty of time for a brisk walk to clear her head of her dark fears for Julie. She would tell Mike about her arrest when he got here. With a smile on her face at the thought of being comforted by Mike, she shuffled her boots through the parking lot to the cleared street. The snow had slowed to a light dusting that collected on her shoulders.

She had gone only a few blocks when her cell rang again. It was Eddie.

"Hey, it's a beautiful day," he said, his voice a little too loud in her ear.

"For sled dogs. Did you lose power?"

"Heck no. I'm in a strip mall. They're not gonna lose power. Speaking of power, wanna go on a power walk with me? I like to walk whenever I can. The gym's fine for bad weather, but there's nothing like fresh air."

Power walking with Eddie was about the last thing on earth she wanted to do. She thought quickly. "I'd like that, but—"

"I'll be right over."

"No, I can't. Eddie?" He was gone. She had planned to say she would like to, *but* she couldn't. Because, well, maybe because she had just gone for a walk.

She tried to call Eddie back, but he didn't answer. Great. Just great. She'd have to get rid of him before Mike came over. She had thought the last thing she wanted to do was go on a power walk with Eddie, but now she'd changed her mind. The last thing she wanted to do was to have both Mike and Eddie in the same spot at the same time.

SEVENTEEN

S he hurried toward home, hoping she could intercept Eddie and send him on his way quickly. He was too fast for her. His bright yellow Smart car was idling outside the door, the exhaust plumes swirling in a mad dance with the lazy snowflakes. For a moment she contemplated turning around and disappearing until he left. As she was formulating the thought, the car door opened. He'd spotted her.

"Hey, Chase! You started without me?"

She waded through the deep accumulation as fast as she could, out of breath by the time she got to him. "I tried to tell you," she said between pants. "I've already walked today. You hung up too quick."

"Aw, gee, that's too bad. Why don't we go over to my shop for a drink?"

She suppressed a shudder at the vision of a glass of green, viscous goo. "I can't. Really. I have too much to do."

"No problem. I'll call earlier in the day next time. You gonna be open tomorrow? Maybe we could meet up then."

"We should be open. The roads are being plowed and the snow is stopping."

"I gotta be getting back anyway. It's been busy today."

With all this snow? Maybe his roads had been plowed earlier than hers. She breathed out a sigh of relief as he ducked to tuck himself into his tiny car. Then he straightened up.

"I forgot. I was gonna tell you that Monique Byrd came into the shop today. That woman is crazy."

"How so?" She talked a lot and stuck with Dickie, which made her halfway crazy already as far as Chase was concerned.

"She has a weird thing about not touching people. She won't let anyone touch her skin."

Chase remembered that from high school, but it had seemed worse the few times she'd seen her lately. "She has a germ phobia."

"And that means she's crazy in my book. Normal people don't mind touching each other."

He put his ungloved hand on her cheek. Startled, Chase pulled away. The gesture seemed too intimate. She did get giddy in his presence, but there was all that emphasis on health food and he didn't seem to like Quincy very much.

"Different people have different obsessions," she said. *Some are obsessed with quinoa sprouts.* "Look, I have to get going." She resisted glancing at the time on her phone.

"Sure." He shrugged and got into his car again. "See you around."

Was that a brush-off? After his car disappeared, she lifted her hand and felt her cheek, tingling and warm where his hand had been.

She was still standing with her ratty glove to her face when Mike's extended-cab pickup came around the corner. He pulled up to where she was standing—after she had whipped her hand down to her side.

"Are you waiting out here to meet me?" His grin, with his raised eyebrows, was curious.

"I'm returning from a walk."

"In this weather?"

"What can I say? I love shuffling through the snow."

He got out of the truck holding plastic bag. "You love shuffling through leaves, too. Is it shuffling you like? You'll make a great old person."

She had to laugh. "Do you know anything about your power?"

"The phone message says there's a major failure in the western suburbs that includes the Minnetonka Mills area. They didn't promise it will be on any sooner than tomorrow when I called the recording. The condo might get power earlier. They're not saying. It's so close to here, you're lucky yours didn't go out."

Chase led the way inside. She paused halfway across the kitchen floor when she heard voices out front. No one should be there now. The shop was closed and everyone had left.

"I thought you had closed," Mike said, echoing her thoughts.

She held a finger to her lips to shush him so she could listen before she went out there.

"I could get you disqualified, you know." That was Grace Pilsen, she was sure, her voice dripping with vitriol. How did she get inside the Bar None? "You'll get thrown out of the Minny Batter Battle."

"You just now said this isn't the recipe you're using." Anna was here! And she was angry.

Chase motioned for Mike to follow. He stuck his bag into the fridge first. Together, they pushed through the swinging doors.

Anna and Grace were standing at the front door. Grace waved a piece of familiar-looking paper in Anna's face, but Anna stood her ground, her arms folded and her chin out.

"What's going on?" Chase asked.

When Grace whirled toward her, the venom she shot at Chase was so virulent that Chase was very glad Mike was beside her.

"I suppose you helped her steal my recipe."

Chase shrank away involuntarily. As Chase feared, she held the copy that Patrice had made.

"I had nothing to do with taking that," Chase said. "And neither did Anna." She felt her own anger rising. Who did this woman think she was, attacking Anna that way?

"I don't believe that for a minute," Grace said with a sneer. She gave a mighty sneeze and Chase noticed how red her nose was. "How did this get into the bag of dessert bars my assistant bought here Thursday?"

How did it? Chase frowned, trying to puzzle it out. She

had put it into the pocket of her smock. Then she had gone out front to work. "What does your assistant look like?"

"What does that matter?" Grace took a threatening step toward Chase. She sneezed again, this time in Chase's face.

Chase could feel Mike close behind her. "I'm trying to figure this out. It was in my pocket. Do you have a cold? Would you like a tissue?" She felt like washing her face immediately, but that wasn't possible.

"What's important is how did *you* get it?" Grace's red nose was almost touching Chase's. It was raw, probably from wiping.

"A well-meaning person thought we would like to see the recipe," Chase said, taking a step away from Grace's germs. She wasn't going to drag Patrice into Grace's sights. "That person brought it to me. I scolded her for doing it and never showed it to Anna. If you've shown it to her, that's the first she's seen of it."

Grace squinted at Chase, probably not buying any of her story. Mike stepped up beside Chase.

"Wait a minute," Chase added. "Didn't everyone have to turn in their recipes already? A week ago, wasn't it?"

Grace nodded.

Anna gave Chase an appreciative smile. "I see what you're saying," she said.

"It doesn't make one bit of difference who knows what now," Chase went on. "The ingredients are finalized. You can't make any changes now."

"If you want me to," Anna said with a smug grin, "I'll show you my recipe."

"I could easily deconstruct all your recipes from our

samples. They're not very complicated." Grace gave a huff and stalked out the front door. She climbed into her car, which sat at the curb. Anna's blue Volvo was parked behind it.

"What just happened?" Chase asked. "What are you doing here and what was *she* doing here?"

"I forgot to bring home Inger's smock. I told her I'd make the ties longer to accommodate her baby bump as it grows. When I got here, I saw *that Grace Pilsen's* car out front and—big mistake—let her in when she followed me to the front door."

"Maybe she didn't know we closed today for the snow," Chase said.

"No, she thought we were open. She waltzed in right behind me."

"You have a sign on the door," Mike pointed out. "It says you're closed."

"Who knows what goes on in that woman's mind?" Anna picked up Inger's smock, which was sitting on one of the round display tables where she had set it when she opened the door. She stuffed it into her purse and headed out. "I'll see you later, Charity," she called with a wave.

Mike shook his head. "What was that all about?"

"Besides being exposed to a nasty cold? I can't figure out how her assistant got the recipe. It had to have made its way into a bag of dessert bars somehow."

"Why was she—or he—here buying your products?"

"Probably wanted to see how good they are. I don't think Grace has ever had anything from our place." Chase leaned against the glass case. It was empty and the lights were off, the glass polished, waiting for the shop to reopen on Monday.

"I must have fished something out of my pocket, a pencil or even a tissue, and didn't notice that the recipe copy came out of my pocket. I'll have to ask Mallory and Inger if they remember anything about it."

At least Mike didn't ask any more questions. She didn't want to tell him his cousin was pilfering for her and Anna.

EIGHTEEN

If Chase had to be shut up somewhere during a snowstorm, inside her own apartment, cuddling with Dr. Michael Ramos, was a good place to be. He had obviously planned his foray to her refrigerator, because he dashed out to his car before he came upstairs and returned with a naturally chilled bottle of burgundy.

The two of them, joined by a purring tabby cat, watched the snow fall from her leather couch, wrapped in an afghan Anna had made for her last Christmas, as they sipped the dark, ruby goodness and munched on a few toffee dessert bars. The snow had picked up again and was now thicker and faster than ever.

After the snowplows made a second trip down Chase's street, Mike thought he'd better get going before the streets filled up with snow again. "I'd love to stay much longer, but I should leave now." He gazed into her face for a long moment. She searched his eyes, wondering how deep his feelings for her went. She thought she saw flickers of love, but wasn't sure.

"You won't have any trouble with that big truck, will you?" Chase asked.

"Probably not, but this isn't going to let up anytime soon."

She had to agree with that. It was on the tip of her tongue to suggest he stay the night, but he gave her a peck on the cheek and left before she could form the right phrase in her mind. How do you ask that, she wondered. Everything she thought of sounded wrong: Wanna stay over? Would you like to stay here? Are you sure you want to leave?

Back on the couch, she was left with a cozy, warm glow. Part of it was the wine, but part was from the warmth of a big, strong man, whose arm had been around her for an hour. The only part that bothered her was the chaste peck he gave her when he left. It wasn't a kiss, a real kiss. Was he pulling away from her? Was he interested in someone else?

She wandered downstairs to work on the billing for the shop, since she had all this extra time. Switching on her monitor, she breathed a sigh of relief that it was working. At least she hadn't lost power. Quincy padded after her and curled up on the floor beside her.

This was where they were supposed to be now. The cat was content. He had been puzzled when everyone left the shop in the middle of the day. He was disappointed now that

there were no baking smells coming from the kitchen. None of the women who slipped him tidbits were around. He missed them. This one, although she made delicious treats and din dins, never let loose with extras between scheduled meals and treats. She was rigid that way. He had enjoyed nestling with her and his vet upstairs, but it felt normal to be here in the office. He checked under the desk. The paper and his other treasures were where he had left them. He was too warm and comfy to make the effort of batting at any of them. Maybe some other time.

Julie called when Chase was in the middle of paying some vendors online. *What did businesses ever do before computers and the Internet?*

"Have they plowed your street?" Julie asked.

"Twice. They don't usually do that."

"It's almost stopped snowing here."

"It keeps starting and stopping. Have you seen the weather forecast?" Chase clicked over to the weather site as she said it.

"This should be the end of it," she said. "I talked to Anna. She said you closed up early. What've you been doing?"

Julie was trying to sound casual, so Chase chuckled.

"Oh, Mike came over, I'll bet."

"He lost power and asked me to refrigerate some insulin for his boarders. And he stayed awhile."

"Nice."

"What are you doing?"

"Jay and I were at his place. We talked about my . . . my case." Julie's voice faltered on the last word. If only she didn't have a case!

"Does he have any insight? Any words of wisdom?" Chase turned an invoice over on her desk and started in on the next one.

"Not really. But he trusts Gerrold that there's not enough evidence to go forward."

"Then why are they even still considering you?"

"I guess because they don't have anybody else. Do you have dinner plans?"

"If Jay is gone, why don't you bring Chinese over here? I'm doing some computer work that will take me about an hour."

They had a companionable evening, but Chase was frustrated when Julie left. She didn't have as much faith as Julie did in her lawyer. She had a lot more experience with Detective Niles Olson than she did with Gerrold Gustafson and didn't think he and the district attorney would be bringing the case to a grand jury unless they thought there was a chance of pinning the murder on her best friend.

Sunday morning dawned extra bright. The sun reflected off the snow outside onto Chase's bedroom wall and woke her fifteen minutes before her alarm was set to go off at eight o'clock. She'd had a bad night, lying awake worrying about Julie and wondering if there was anything she could do. At one point she considered going to the police station and talking to the detective. Then she drifted into a restless sleep and dreamed that she found a bloody knife, thus exonerating Julie. It was a light sleep and she awoke from the dream, realizing that there was no knife involved. Her despair descended with even more weight.

The phone startled her minutes after she opened her bleary eyes to the overly bright sunshine. She picked up her cell. It was Eddie. She let it go to voice mail, but he immediately called again, so she answered.

"You up for a jog today?"

"Eddie, our shop is open on Sundays."

"We could get one in quick, before you open. The snow stopped."

Was the man made of energy? "No, we could not. I'm still in bed."

"Really? What is it, eight?"

He probably got up at five. "Not yet. My alarm will go off when it's eight."

"How about after work?"

It would be dark when the shop closed at six. She felt she was being rude. She did enjoy being around him, if they weren't eating cardboard health food and if he wasn't berating her about the contents of her dessert bars. "Maybe Monday. We're closed Monday and Tuesday." That would give her a day to think of an alternative activity to jogging on snowy, slushy sidewalks.

"Call me Monday, then?"

She promised she would. Should she feel bad about seeing two men at once? No, she told herself. It wasn't like she was committed to either one. And vice versa, as far as she could tell.

Before she finished breakfast she heard Anna arrive and *yoo-hoo* up the stairs to let her know she was at work. She stumbled down the stairs, feeling the lack of sleep. Quincy darted in front of her at the bottom of the steps and she nearly tripped over him.

"Are you okay?" Anna asked.

"A little tired. I didn't sleep well last night."

"Worried about Julie?"

When Chase nodded, Anna confessed that she was, too. If she had spent a sleepless night over Julie, it didn't show. She wore a bright blue, green, and red cardigan over a pink T-shirt. The theme was trees. Not strictly Christmas trees, but pine trees with red and blue bows. Appropriate for the season. Anna's cheeks were the pink of her shirt and her eyes blazed blue to match the yarn of the bows in the bright daylight flooding the kitchen. The kitchen faced east and the windows, kept clean mostly by Anna, let all the December light in. Chase wished there were some warmth with the light, but it *was* December.

Inspecting Anna more closely in the light, she could detect dark smudges beneath those sparkling eyes.

"I have to look something up," Chase said. "Be right back."

She followed Quincy into the office and searched for current movies to try to find one Eddie might be interested in. Although she had no idea what his taste in movies was, she could probably rule out chick flicks. Would he go for the he-man thriller stuff? There was a new James Bond. Maybe he'd like that. She made a note of times and theaters for all the shows that were possibilities. The one thing she wasn't going to do was jog in December after a snowstorm. She wasn't even big on jogging on dry pavement in good weather. She did love biking, but this was no longer the time of year for that.

When Mallory and Inger had both arrived, she talked to them in the kitchen before they opened the shop.

"This is a long shot, I know, but do either of you remember if you sold anything to someone who works with Grace Pilsen?"

They looked at each other.

"Pilsen?" Mallory asked.

"Does this have anything to do with something called The Pilsener?" Inger said.

"Yes," Chase said. "That's the shop Grace owns. You remember something about it?"

They both nodded.

"How could we forget?" Inger said. "This woman came in and said she wanted to buy one of each bar—everything we sell."

"And she paid with a credit card from a place called The Pilsener," Mallory added. "I thought the woman probably owned a bar."

"It's actually a bakery," Chase said.

They both shook their heads. "I wondered what a tavern would do with so many dessert bars," Mallory said.

"It was so weird," Inger said. "We told her we didn't sell every single type every single day, so she bought everything we had on hand. I've been expecting her to come back another day and do it again, but she hasn't."

"You don't remember sticking an extra piece of paper in the bag, do you?"

"Bags. There were several of them."

Chase thanked them and they went out front with her to fill the cases while Chase tended the cash register and flipped the sign to "Open."

So that was how Grace thought she could "deconstruct" the Bar None recipes, Chase mused. It was unlikely that she could, but she at least knew most of their products if she'd bought nearly each type of bar. That must have been how the purloined recipe copy got to her, too. Chase could envision it falling out of her apron pocket and landing on the shelf under the counter that held the paper bags. Sometimes her pencil fell out of her pocket and that's where it landed if it didn't hit the floor. She was sorry she hadn't seen it before it got into Grace's purchase.

On the way to the kitchen, she yawned and stretched, trying to stay wide-awake.

Chase and Anna baked most of the morning, then relieved the salesclerks as they had their lunches. After Chase came back and sent Inger to the front, she decided to do some more ordering. The cinnamon was nearly gone and they used a lot this time of year.

No sooner had she sat at her desk, with Quincy purring in her lap, than the office phone rang.

It was Detective Olson. For a split second, her tired brain thought she had called him, but then remembered that she had formed the idea and rejected it. So what was he calling about?

"Ms. Oliver?" She sat up straighter. He called her Chase

when he wasn't being official and formal. "We need you to come to the station to answer a few more questions. Could you make it this afternoon?"

At least he let her set the time. Sort of. "Yes, sure, I can come anytime. What is this about?"

"About the murder. About you finding the body."

Holy smokes! Was the next suspect . . . Chase Oliver?

NINETEEN

Detective Niles Olson had taken Chase on a mental trip through discovering a body before and it had almost been like hypnotism. While sitting at the chair beside his desk, she had recalled details that had escaped her previously. It didn't work this time, though.

"You saw the scarf beside the body like this, right?" He had sketched in the way it had lain on the dirt beside Ron's body, still partly around his neck.

Yes, it was exactly as she had told him the last time she was questioned.

"No footprints in the mud? Any drag marks?"

"No, only Quincy sitting there eating some peanuts that must have been in Ron's pocket. Would his head have made drag marks?" His head had been toward the street and his feet farther into the bush, so if he were dragged, it had to have been by his feet. The detective had told her Ron North was killed somewhere else. Something about knowing the body had been moved.

"Probably not. But after both Dr. Ramos and you were crawling around in there, we don't have any good prints from the dirt."

Chase thought that could not have been helped. They had to crawl into the bush to find him.

"And you're sure his blackmail victims didn't kill him? Alone or together? Hail and Snelson are in on that shady deal together, trying to cheat people by buying up their property for less than it's worth."

"Those two spent the night together at Mr. Snelson's house. That's backed up by his wife. She insists her husband came home very soon after the reunion."

That woman had made a point of telling Mike Ramos, too. The fact that she was reiterating the story all over town made Chase doubt that it was true. "And Hail was with him? Why would he sleep at their house?"

The detective frowned. Was he getting impatient with her questions? "They both say they had business to discuss pertaining to their new real estate venture and needed to work on it that night. They walked to Snelson's house, which is nearby."

"Their scam, you mean. That would be hard to do since they were both drunk. Mrs. Snelson told me, when she came into the shop yesterday, that her husband didn't come home that night. She did say he spent the night with Mr. Hail, but not at her house."

He scribbled something on his notepad. "Looks like we need to talk to Mrs. Snelson once more."

"How about Mr. Snelson? And Mr. Hail, too? Why would Mr. Hail spend the night at anyone's house? That would be odd, since he lives in town, doesn't he?"

Olson didn't answer any of her questions, but she knew they were good ones.

Maybe she would try to talk to the men herself. These people were changing stories every day. If she collected enough contradictions, Olson would take them seriously and Julie's charges could be dropped and her hearing could be canceled.

After Chase returned to the shop, Mrs. Cray, the janitor from Hammond High School, came into the Bar None again. Chase happened to be behind the counter when she paid for her purchase, six Margarita Cheesecake Bars.

"I can't resist," she said. "I do love a margarita. Not that often, every once in a blue moon. Not that often at all." She got her checkbook out and started writing. "Now, what's the date? Oh, it's Sunday, isn't it? Maybe I shouldn't eat these on Sunday."

"There's hardly any alcohol in them, Mrs. Cray," Chase said. "It's there for flavoring, that's all." She didn't mention the tequila and Grand Marnier since all but the taste baked out.

"To think that only last Sunday I was working at Hammond. And there was Mr. Snelson, sound asleep on the couch in his office." She chuckled.

"He . . . slept in his office after the reunion?"

"I'd say he did. He had on a suit—for sure he slept in

it—wrinkled like all get out." She leaned over the counter to whisper to Chase. "That office was a mess, too. I'd say he and the missus are having problems, wouldn't you?"

Chase shrugged. There were more likely explanations, she thought. A missus who alibied her husband probably wasn't kicking him out of the bedroom. Neither of her two versions matched this one. She'd told Chase and Anna that her husband hadn't come home, but had spent the night with Langton Hail. But she'd told the detective that both men spent the night at her house. She was trying hard to give her husband an alibi, it seemed, but wasn't doing a good job of it.

Mrs. Cray stood up straight to deliver the details. "He was all embarrassed and got up real quick. He was rubbing his eyes and yawning. His eyes were red and itchy-looking and he'd thrown tissues all over the floor. What a mess. Said he slept in his office all night so no one would break in. Just because they broke into the junior high school across town doesn't mean he needs to sleep in his office."

The woman leaned in close again for her next condemnation. "I'll tell you what. He smelled like liquor, too. That man had been drinking."

That was true. She'd seen him at the punch bowl getting lacings from Ron North. He'd been embellishing Snelson's drink as well as Hail's with the bourbon from his flask. "There was punch at the reunion."

"There was also a half-empty whiskey bottle on his desk."

"Mrs. Cray, you should tell Detective Olson about this. About where Mr. Snelson was. He needs this information."

"Oh, I couldn't."

"Yes, you have to." She had a thought. "Do you think anyone else spent the night there with him?" Like maybe Langton Hail.

"Oh no, there's only room for one person to sleep there."

Chase wrote Detective Olson's phone number, which she had memorized a long time ago, on the back of Mrs. Cray's receipt. "Here, please call him. He's a good guy. Niles Olson. He needs to know this."

If she didn't tell him about Snelson's odd sleeping habits, Chase would.

Bart Fender came in a couple of hours later, while Chase was again in the front room. This time she was giving Inger her lunch break.

"Raspberry Chiffon again?" Chase asked.

"How do you remember that?"

Chase didn't say that it was stuck in her mind because it seems such a delicate, dainty choice for a high school coach and former wrestler. She shrugged. "I just do. I remember lots of our customers' favorites." That part, at least, was true.

"Julie and I are thinking of going to visit Dillon on Monday. Do you think that would be a good idea?" She was putting out a feeler for how conscious the poor woman was.

"So Julie heard what I said. That would be great! She would love it. Hardly anyone comes by. Her family is there a lot, and me, but that's about it."

"So she recognizes you?"

He looked away. "I'm not sure. But she reacts when she hears my voice. I think she knows it's me."

"She's not really in a coma?"

He screwed his face up into an angry scowl. "No, she's not. She's not in any coma. She's only asleep."

Chase guessed that she and Julie would have to go find out for themselves.

As he left, Bart almost plowed over the next woman to enter the shop. It was none other than Mrs. Snelson. Chase wondered if the woman's ears had been burning earlier when Mrs. Cray and she were talking about her.

"I can take over, Ms. Oliver," Inger said, coming up behind her. Inger had taken a brief potty break.

"Call me Chase, Inger. I can stay out here a little longer."

"It's not that busy. Anna told me to send you to the kitchen. I think she needs some help."

Chase left, frowning. She would much rather stay in the front and talk to Mrs. Snelson again. There was no graceful way to do it, so back to the kitchen she went.

The center island was stacked with boxes.

"The paper delivery came and I have to stir this caramel," Anna said. "Could you clear off a space for me to set a couple of baking sheets so I can pour this?"

"I'll do better than that," Chase said. "I'll put them all away." She got busy stowing the boxes on the lower shelves and the task was done in a few minutes. She straightened from shoving the last box in place, pulled out the pans, and dusted off her hands. "Let me have a look out front for a minute," she said, and dashed to the front.

She saw Mrs. Snelson going out the door. Oh well. If the woman was becoming a regular, there would be another time soon to talk to her and see if she had yet another story about the night of the reunion.

At Mallory's next break, Chase sat with her while Anna took her place selling.

"Did Mrs. Snelson buy the same thing this time?" Chase asked.

Mallory frowned. "Just the Lemon Bars. I asked her if she would like Peanut Butter Fudge again, but she started on a rant about her husband."

That was interesting. "What sort of rant?"

"She called him some bad names and said she wasn't buying anything for him ever again."

That was certainly puzzling. Mrs. Cray thought the marriage was in trouble, but Mrs. Snelson had gone to great, if contradictory, lengths to shield her husband from suspicion. Now, however, it seemed Mrs. Cray was right. Maybe the relationship was volatile. Would she quit protecting him now?

Chase went to the office to call Detective Niles Olson.

TWENTY

"Why doesn't that man ever answer his phone?" Chase slammed the office phone onto the charger.

When she stormed out of the office Anna asked her what was the matter.

"I wanted to tell Detective Olson something about Mr. Snelson's alibi. It's coming unpeeled like phyllo dough."

"Hm," Anna mused. "What would a baklava dessert bar taste like? How hard would that be?"

"Not now! You have to concentrate on the Minny Batter Battle."

"I know, I know. It's good to be thinking ahead, don't you think?" Anna stopped stirring for a moment. "What about Mr. Snelson?"

"His wife gave him two conflicting alibis, but she was

in just now and Mallory says she bad-mouthed him. She made it clear that she's not buying dessert bars for him ever again. That woman likes to tell her business to everyone, I guess, even almost complete strangers."

"I saw his wife this morning," Anna said.

"Mrs. Snelson? Here?"

"No, on my way to work, she was stopped at the light beside me. I recognized her from coming into the shop, but she didn't seem to remember seeing me."

"Did she look guilty of murder?"

"Something is up with that couple. Her backseat was stacked to the roof with piles of stuff."

"Papers?"

Anna cocked her head. "I'd say more like clothing. It looked like men's clothing, dumped into the backseat."

"Wow. I wonder if she kicked Mr. Snelson out. Mallory said she sounded steamed at him."

"I was thinking that might be it."

"Now I really need to get hold of Niles Olson."

"Maybe he doesn't work on Sundays."

Anna was probably right. The man needed a day off once in a while. Even if that was inconvenient for her.

Monday morning, Julie called to set up a time to see Dillon Yardley in the hospital. "I just found out I can get away for an hour at lunchtime," she said. "Meet you there instead of later?"

Chase had slept in that morning. The stress was tiring her out. She hadn't fallen asleep until after two, tossing and turning and worrying. Then, when her alarm rang, she'd hit snooze for an hour.

But she was waiting in the lobby of the hospital at a quarter to twelve, which was good because Julie showed up a bit early. Chase carried a bouquet of carnations and a card, which Julie signed. "You have the room number?" Julie asked.

"I called up there as soon as I got here. Bart answered the phone. I was so surprised I hung up."

"Oh great, *he's* here." Julie twisted the corner of her mouth. "Oh well. This is the only time I have until late today."

"He's not my favorite person either, but I think his heart's in the right place. He's very faithful to Dillon. By the way, he said something about you hearing him when I told him we would visit Dillon."

Julie shook her head. "That's what he wanted legal advice about in the parking lot."

"About Dillon?"

"Yes. It's complicated."

The elevator dinged when they reached Dillon's floor and they wound through the hallways to get to the room. They peeked in.

"Is this the right number?" Julie whispered. "It's full of people."

"There's Bart, over by the window."

The room was small and held three large visitors. Bart Fender was one of them. His thick body blocked half the light from the window. The other two, an older couple, sat in chairs on the other side of the bed. The man held the hand of the frail, pale woman in the bed. Her skin was nearly as white as the sheets. Faint blue veins crisscrossed her temples. Dillon had always been fair, but now it looked as though her skin was transparent, stretched tight across the bones of her face and hands.

"We have to, young man," the older man said to Bart. "And we're going to. It needs to be done and there's nothing you can do about it."

"I can go to a judge. I'll bring an injunction. You can't kill her." Bart spoke through clenched teeth, his hands tightly fisted at his sides. Intense pain showed in his narrowed eyes.

The older man released Dillon's inert hand and rose from his chair. "You have no legal standing here, Fender. She's our daughter. And she's not going to get better."

"You don't know that! She could! She only needs to wake up." Bart's eyes squeezed together and his tears streamed down his cheeks to his thick neck. "You don't talk to her enough."

Chase realized he had been crying all along.

Bart noticed them at that moment. "What are you doing here?" He sounded belligerent.

"Don't you remember I said I would come and visit Dillon?" Chase asked.

He gave a slight nod. "Oh. Yeah."

"Maybe now isn't a good time," Julie said.

"I'm sorry." The woman stood and extended a hand. "We haven't met. I'm Dillon's mother."

Chase and Julie introduced themselves to Dillon's parents. Mrs. Yardley took the flowers and the card and propped them up alongside a few others on the wide windowsill. "Bart said he thought Dillon would like some visitors," Chase said.

"I'm so sorry," Dillon's mother said. "Her father and I have decided to . . ."

"They're going to pull the plug," Bart shouted. "They're going to kill her."

"Bart, be reasonable." Dillon's mother gestured to him with her palm outstretched. "The doctors say her brain is severely damaged." She looked at Bart, pleading with her sad eyes. "It's time, Bart."

"I'll stop this. You'll see." He stormed out past all of them, brushing against Chase roughly as he left the room. She could feel heat emanating from him, he was so angry.

"Oh dear." Dillon's mother's face puckered. "Can he really do that? Stop us from letting her go?"

Chase turned to Julie. Julie shrugged. She obviously didn't know if he'd be able to or not. That was probably what he'd wanted Julie to give him legal advice about. A look passed between the parents that told Chase she was right.

"Is she completely unresponsive?" Chase asked.

"What Bart sees," said Dillon's father, "are some reflexive movements. Some occasional jerking. The hospital doctor is no help. He won't explain it to Bart. But if her brain is damaged, she has no chance. There's no point in continuing life support. Our own family doctor agrees with us."

"Not in so many words," his wife said, rearranging the cards on the windowsill.

"No, but that's what he meant. He said he wouldn't continue if it were his daughter."

Chase shuddered at the stark words. The agony was palpable in this warm, small room. She reached out and touched the hands of Dillon's parents, unable to speak. Julie did the same, and they departed in silence.

Julie had to say good-bye in the parking garage so she could get back to work. Chase drove home slowly, bothered by the terrible decision Dillon's parents were forced to make. Bart, she was convinced, was positive he was doing the right thing, but he was making it harder for Dillon's parents. There was no good solution. When she got home, she cuddled with Quincy and watched traffic from inside her balcony doors until she felt a bit calmer. Then she called Detective Olson.

"Olson here." He sounded official and in a hurry.

"This is Chase Oliver, Detective Olson."

"Chase, you can call me Niles, you know." His voice softened.

Sometimes she thought she could, but at other times she didn't think so. "Okay, Niles. I wanted you to know that Mrs. Cray, the janitor at the high school, was in our shop yesterday. Has she called you?"

"No. What about?" Now he was interested.

"She cleaned the school Sunday morning after the reunion and she found the principal asleep in his office. She thought Mr. Snelson had slept there all night." *And left tissues all over the floor.*

"Do you have a number for her?"

Chase mentally kicked herself. "No, I gave her your number."

"I don't think that helped, did it? She hasn't called me."

He didn't have to rub it in and make her feel even worse for not thinking of getting some information from the woman.

"It's all right, Chase. I can find her. As a matter of fact, I interviewed Mrs. Snelson again this morning and she finally told us what I'm pretty sure is the truth. It also matches what your janitor says."

"Which truth did she tell this time?" How could he be sure when she had given so many versions?

"She broke down, said she told him to leave the house and drove all his clothes to the dump. She said he had urged her to lie for him, but she hated doing it. She apparently didn't know he was involved with the land swindle that's been in the news. He told her about it a couple of nights ago and she blew up at him."

"That makes sense. Anna said she saw Mrs. Snelson's car yesterday and it was piled high with clothing."

"We re-interviewed him after talking with his wife and he gave us the same story. He slept all night at the school. The reason he didn't go home after the reunion was that he's allergic to his wife's new dog. She's been lying to protect him from being a murder suspect, but she's pretty upset about the real estate thing."

"I think he had a lot to drink." Mrs. Cray had said he smelled like liquor the next day. Chase herself had seen him taking hits from Ron's flask around the punch bowl, too. Maybe Ron compensated his blackmail victims with shots of fortification.

"He admitted he was being blackmailed by Mr. North," Niles said. "But I don't think he could have killed him. A few witnesses say he was almost too drunk to stand by the end of the evening. We have two, now three, matching accounts of his whereabouts."

"Should you be telling me all of this?"

"I just talked to a reporter and gave her most of the same information. Enough to publicly get Snelson off the hook anyway."

"I didn't know he was *on* the hook. I thought Julie was the only one there."

"Definitely not the only one."

"But she is still on?"

"Yep. She's still on."

TWENTY-ONE

C hase felt more despondent than ever. Julie was firmly in the sights of Detective Olson for Ron North's murder. Another cuddling session with Quincy didn't lift her spirits. Maybe she would take her kitty out on his leash. Some fresh air and exercise might be what she needed to sharpen her mind about who had actually killed the reporter.

"Let's go, little guy." She got his leash off the hook by her door where she'd been keeping it.

He padded over to her, which made her smile. Maybe, she thought, he's getting used to the leash. My training is working.

Before she realized where they were heading, she found herself in front of the neighborhood tavern, standing in the very spot where Dickie Byrd had been kissing the woman who was not Monique, his wife. She wanted to stop a moment to think about things, but Quincy wanted to keep moving. The sidewalks everywhere were shoveled and dry. A squirrel scolded Quincy from halfway down the trunk of a tree planted in the sidewalk.

"You won't catch him, you know," she said to Quincy.

"Won't catch who?" a man's low voice said.

Chase turned in time see a short man stagger out the door. His overcoat was open, showing his plaid vest. Langton Hail must have overheard her comment.

"Are you talking to me?" he asked. "I'm not trying to catch anyone." His words were slurred and he grabbed the trunk of the tree, right where the squirrel had been, to steady himself. The squirrel scampered to the topmost branches and quit chattering.

"No, I . . . My cat . . ."

The man was a lot drunker than she'd seen him either the night of the reunion or at the restaurant where she'd been with Eddie.

"What're you lookin' at?" His body swayed toward her.

"Sorry, Mr. Hail. I'm out walking my cat. Do you need some help?"

"Who you think you are? I don't need any help. How do you know me anyway? Get outta my way."

Chase was glad to oblige him and walked briskly down the sidewalk. When she reached the corner, she glanced behind. Langton Hail was still clutching the tree, reeling in an attempt to stay upright. He didn't seem to have any idea who she was, but why would he? She was one of the many alums at the reunion and he'd been an outsider, easy for everyone to notice. His code name, PHOTO, in Ron North's notebook, had one less numerical entry beside it than PRINCE, Mr. Snelson's code name, and she hadn't seen anything pass between those two that night. Had Hail refused to pay Ron North? Had they had an altercation later, maybe when Ron attempted to extort the money? Had it ended up with Ron dead? And that's why the man was drinking so much. Remorse and guilt. Trying to wipe out the memory of what he'd done.

She hoped Hail was firmly in Detective Olson's sights along with Julie. He belonged there. Julie didn't.

When she got home and released Quincy from his harness, she gave him a warm Kitty Patty and told him what a good boy he was. Then, after pacing her kitchen for a few minutes, she called Anna.

She sat in her cushy chair and stared out at the street below. It was mid afternoon but, this far north, the sun was setting and it was already beginning to get dark. Anna's phone rang and rang. As Chase decided she wasn't going to answer, Anna picked it up. She sounded sleepy.

"Did I wake you?" Chase asked. "Were you taking a nap?"

"Not a nap. I closed my eyes for a few minutes."

Yeah, right, Chase thought. It was that kind of day, chilly and gray, a good day for napping. In fact, her voice sounded like she was awakening from a sound sleep.

"You aren't practicing for the baking contest?"

Anna's sigh came over the phone with a *whoosh*. "I can't."

"What's wrong?" Chase sat up straight. "Why can't you?" There was an air of defeat in Anna's tone that Chase had seldom heard.

"I mean I don't think I need to. I'm ready. Practicing more won't make me any better."

"Are you ready to beat Grace Pilsen?"

"Who knows?"

That wasn't like Anna. "Anna, don't be discouraged. You probably don't need to rehearse anymore. You've got this in the bag."

"I'm not discouraged, Charity," she snipped. That wasn't like her, either. She was discouraged, Chase just knew it. "Is that why you called? To make sure I'm working on my entry?"

"No, actually. I called about a couple of things. I wanted to tell you that the principal, Mr. Snelson, is no longer a suspect for Ron North's murder."

"Does anyone know why I saw his wife driving around with all those clothes in her car?"

"I told Niles about that. He says Mr. Snelson's wife kicked him out when he told her he was involved in the land swindle. Then she admitted to the police that he hadn't been home that night. Detective Olson has decided he slept at the high school all night. The janitor confirms that. She saw him waking up on his couch the next morning."

"Where does that leave Julie?"

"Still in the bull's-eye, unfortunately. But I also need to tell you about seeing our classmate in the hospital. Julie and I went there at lunchtime."

"Oh yes, Julie said you were going to. I haven't talked to her today. How is the poor girl?"

"She . . . Her parents were there. They want to take her off life support. They don't think she can recover, or that she'll be brain damaged if she does. The hospital doctors don't agree, but their family doctor seems to."

"Oh dear!" Now Anna sounded like herself, alert and concerned. "What exactly happened to her?"

"She tried suicide, from what I heard at the reunion. It didn't kill her, but put her into a coma. She's been unconscious for weeks. She's being kept alive by machines. It's so sad. She was a bouncy, happy person when I knew her a few years ago."

"You know," Anna said, "people sometimes come out of comas. They wake up after years, and some of them are even normal after that."

"Her parents are ready to pull the plug."

"How awful."

"What makes it worse is that Bart Fender opposes them."

"Who is he?"

"He was in our class, too. A wrestler back then. And now he's a coach at Hammond High. He's Dillon's boyfriend and believes she can recover."

"What a mess."

Chase agreed wholeheartedly.

"Anna, are you all right? Should I bring over some Chinese?"

"You know, that would be lovely. I do have a lot on my mind. Julie and the Batter Battle."

"And you're getting married in a little over a week."

"I think I'm more ready for that than for anything else."

TWENTY-TWO

Chase was up, barely, when her phone rang on Tuesday, her last day off for the week. She squinted at the caller ID and groaned.

"Hi, Eddie. What are you doing up so early?" She aimed her squint at her bedside alarm clock. Eight o'clock. She had said she would call him, but not this early.

"It's not that early, is it? I was driving into work and saw you walking your cat yesterday. I wondered if I could walk with you today."

"I'm still in bed."

"I'd really like to see you. I remembered something else about the reunion."

Chase stifled another groan. If he had information that

could shed some light on the murder, she should meet him. "I can be ready in an hour." Maybe waiting that long would discourage him. Eight wasn't early, she agreed, unless it was your day off and you were sleeping in.

"No problem. Give me a jingle when you're ready. My new manager is opening for me today." The guy was so dog-gone cheerful and it was way too early for that.

An hour later, bundled against the cold wind, Chase and Quincy in his harness were walking the route to the Meet N Eat with Eddie, the place where they had met for lunch last week. Eddie handed her one of the two hot drinks he'd brought along.

"What is it?" Chase was suspicious. The heavy paper cup bore the words *Health from the Heath Bar* so she knew it might be anything. Maybe a boiled root from Tasmania or an infusion of exotic herbs from the Siberian tundra.

"Hot chocolate." He grinned and took a sip of his.

She eyed the cup, but couldn't tell what was inside, since it had a lid with a drink spout. "Okay. I love hot chocolate." She was sure there wouldn't be any marshmallows. She took a sip. There wasn't any chocolate either. It was carob.

"Thanks, Eddie." She decided to hold the cup for a few minutes and pretend to sip. For her, a true chocolate lover, carob was nothing but a dirty trick. It was almost chocolate, but not quite. Your nose was fooled until your tongue got the full, deceptive impact.

As they approached the corner before the diner, a familiar pickup truck drove past. It looked very much like Mike Ramos's truck.

Great. Now the morning was perfect. Her sleep-in was

ruined, she was mocked by hot carob, and Mike had seen her taking a walk with Eddie Heath. She probably couldn't pretend this was a business meeting.

She was going to have to make up her mind. Either she kept seeing Eddie Heath or she didn't. The trouble was, her brain knew which decision she should make. But here he was next to her, exuding a distinctly sexy aura, touching her hand when he handed her the cup and sending shock waves through her admittedly weak body. To make everything worse, when he trained those bedroom eyes on her, as he did now when he talked about how well Quincy was doing, she had trouble tearing her gaze away, even to check on her obedient (for a change) cat.

"Hey, look where we are," Eddie said as they approached the front of Meet N Eat.

The morning was very cold and Chase was sorry the place wasn't open yet so they could go in and warm up. They probably wouldn't have let Quincy in, however.

"We saw that drunk guy here," Eddie went on. "Remember? Langton Hail. I wonder if he was ever sober before he started coming into my health bar."

"He visits your place?"

"He started coming a few days ago. I think he's serious about going straight. He's talked to me about his addiction. People do that. They talk to me like I'm a bartender."

"So he's an alcoholic?" Chase wondered if Ron North knew the man had an alcohol addiction. He was giving him shots from the flask. That seemed like cruelty to Chase, tempting the man with his vice. Did Langton Hail get angry about that and kill Ron North?

"That's what he says. He was drunk at the reunion, looked like he was still drunk the next morning, and then—"

"What did you say? What next morning?"

"After the reunion."

"You saw him? Where?"

"I drive past the high school to get to work. I told you I saw a car there? I didn't tell you this part. I didn't know who he was then. But it was Hail in his car the next morning. It looked like he was just waking up, stretching and everything. Like he'd slept in his car there all night."

"You had time to see all that?"

"I was at a red light. When I thought about it, it seemed funny he was still there. He got out and started clearing his windshield, full of snow, as the light turned." Eddie thought for a half a second. "Maybe he wasn't that drunk, then. He was moving well, standing up okay."

"We need to turn around here," Chase said. She wanted to think this out. It wouldn't be good for the detective to get wind of Eddie's story. That would eliminate one more suspect and drive another nail into—not Julie's coffin, exactly, but her murder charge. This was Tuesday and her hearing was Friday. There wasn't much time left to figure out a way to save her best friend from a horrible ordeal, an indictment and a trial.

Then another thought took her a different direction. Why on earth did Langton Hail and Van Snelson bother to alibi each other if they had actual alibis?

"You on a tight schedule?" Eddie's words dripped skepticism.

"Not that. I just remembered something I need to do."

These two stood there talking. That's not how you took a walk, the cat knew. Taking a walk meant moving. It was cold out here and the annoyed tabby wanted to go inside and curl up on the soft chair. He shook himself to keep warm. That was when he noticed that the harness wasn't fastened all the way. He wondered if he could get it off again and return home. He worked at it with his left hind leg, then his right hind leg. It was coming undone. Another little bit and he could start moving.

"Anyway, I think Hail is making a real effort to—" Eddie spun around at the same moment Chase felt the slack on the leash. "Your cat's loose."

"Yes, he certainly is." Chase sighed. "It looks like he might be headed home, at least."

"That would be a first, wouldn't it?" Eddie said, taking off at full speed.

Eddie and Chase scrambled after the fleeing Quincy. A flash of ginger fur disappeared around the corner and they both sped up.

Chase started panting after half a block, but Eddie easily could run another twenty miles.

"You okay?" he asked.

"I'll be fine." It was annoying that she was winded after less than a block.

"You oughta join the gym I belong to. Working out is so good for your body."

Talking while running wasn't helping her at all. They raced down the short end of the block, then rounded another corner.

Chase held out her arm to bring Eddie to a halt. Quincy sat on his haunches half a block away, in front of an apartment building. She didn't want to charge up and make him take off again. Chase held the empty harness tightly in her hand so that it wouldn't jingle and walked slowly toward her cat. Eddie stayed a few steps behind her. She was relieved that he understood what she was doing and followed her lead.

"Hi there, Quincy Wincy," she crooned.

He turned his head toward her, but stayed put.

When she was two feet away, a door opened and he took off.

"Well, hello. Charity Oliver, isn't it?" Dickie Byrd said. He was coming from the apartments. With him was a much younger woman. Chase was pretty sure it was the person she'd seen him kissing a week ago. She was short, with ample curves. Chase hadn't been able to tell how young she was last week at a distance. Dickie's face turned red.

"Hi, Dickie. I have to go get my cat."

"Dickie?" the woman said. "Really?" She looked at him. "Aren't you going to introduce me, Richard?"

Chase hesitated, curious about the two. Dickie didn't say a word. After a brief glare at Chase and a glance at Eddie, he stared at the ground, his lips clamped tight.

"Gotta run," Chase said, and hurried off.

Quincy came to a stop at the end of that block and let Chase put the harness back on. When she had to take off her gloves to make sure she got the harness fastened securely, she realized how cold it was. Her fingers were stiff as she pulled her holey gloves over them.

"Why did he stop?" Eddie asked. Chase noticed that he still wasn't breathing hard. She was panting so much she could barely speak. All that health food probably was good for a person. It just wasn't . . . good.

"Who knows why a cat does anything?" A couple more deep breaths, and she was back to normal.

"I'm telling you, a gym membership is the way to go. You get muscles without that scary steroid bulk."

"What are you talking about?"

"You know. People like Bart Fender. He's got that look. Those lumps between his neck and his shoulders, know what I mean?"

Yes, that's what Bart was like. Lumpy. Very solid lumps, but unnatural.

"What was that all about?" Eddie asked.

"I think I didn't get it fastened all the way. I was in a hurry—"

"No, I meant that business with Dickie Byrd and . . . whoever that was with him."

"I'm not entirely sure."

"He wasn't eager to introduce us, was he?"

"Have you ever seen her before?"

Eddie shook his head. "Maybe she's his niece or something. Looks like she lives in those apartments."

Or something. Chase was sure the voluptuous woman wasn't Dickie Byrd's niece.

TWENTY-THREE

C hase raised her face and closed her eyes, loving the baking aromas that always lingered in the Bar None. It was pleasant to be in the shop when no one else was there. She wandered through the kitchen into the salesroom. Even with the lights off, the clean glass in the display case glinted in the late afternoon light. The pink shelves held boxes of dessert bars, standing at attention and lined up like little pink-striped soldiers. Small round tables held stacked boxes, but the supplies there were low. She would have to remember to have either Inger or Mallory replenish them.

Quincy wound through her legs on her slow amble. It was chilly in the shop with the heat turned down for the day, so his furry rubs felt warm and nice.

She was at loose ends. Maybe she would get some work

done in the office. Sitting at the computer, she pulled up the Bar None webpage to admire the handiwork of Tanner, then opened the screens she needed and got to work.

Chase paused partway through going over her inventory to think about Van Snelson and Langton Hail, the men she had considered the two best suspects for Ron North's murder. They both had perfectly good alibis. The principal, even though he was part of a shady real estate exercise and was being blackmailed by Ron, probably for the real estate swindle, was at the high school all night. Chase had less and less respect for the man. Learning that he actually disliked the students and couldn't stand to be around them contributed to her negative feelings. He might also be skimming money from the school system. But it didn't look like he had murdered Ron.

Langton Hail, because he was also part of the real estate deal, and had probably roped Snelson into it with him, was such a good possibility. He, too, was being blackmailed, if they interpreted the notebook correctly. For the school funds or the real estate deals. But he had slept in his car that night.

So why had they given each other false alibis? Even to the extent of involving Snelson's wife? Chase's best guess on that was because they were trying to keep their true whereabouts hidden for other reasons. Van Snelson didn't want it known yet that he was leaving the high school job. How did that tie in, though? Maybe his marriage was in trouble even then? Divorce seemed to matter more for a school principal than for some other folks. Hail wouldn't want everyone to know that he was an alcoholic and had drunk too much to drive. At least he had the good sense not to take to the road when he was inebriated. Maybe he had lost his license in the past. He was truly trying to fight his addiction, according to Eddie Heath.

There was, she thought, still a slight chance that one of these two crooks had murdered Ron North, but it was becoming less and less likely. So who did that leave?

The name in the notebook under PRINCE (Principal Van Snelson) and PHOTO (real estate developer Langton Hail) was BIRD. Richard "Dickie" Byrd. He hadn't started giving Ron blackmail money yet, it appeared, since no numbers accompanied his code name, but he was on the list. Maybe he was determined not to let himself be blackmailed and refused to fork over money? At this stage of his political career, a mistress wouldn't do him any good. What was Dickie Byrd's alibi?

Did his wife alibi him, too? Was Dickie with her? Would Detective Niles Olson tell her?

There was one way to find out.

He answered his cell phone on the first ring, for once.

"Hi, Chase." He sounded easy and friendly today, not uptight and official, as he sometimes did.

"Detective Olson? Could I ask you a couple of questions?" Quincy, who had been dozing on the floor of the office, decided Chase's lap was too empty. So he jumped into it and bumped his head against her arm, almost jostling the phone out of her hands.

"You can always ask."

"I guess that's right." And he was free to not answer. "I just learned that it was Langton Hail's car in the parking lot Sunday morning."

"Yes, we know that. He admitted leaving his car there when we asked him."

"He was in it."

"He was *in* the car? You saw him?"

"No, Eddie Heath saw him waking up in his car, like he'd been there all night. He didn't know who it was on Sunday. Now Mr. Hail has started going into Eddie's shop and he recognized him."

There was a pause. That was a good sign, Chase thought. The detective was considering her information. "That doesn't exactly jibe with his statement." It sounded like he was talking to himself. "He and Snelson both said they spent the night together at Snelson's house. Hail was too drunk to drive. Snelson's wife backed him up at first, but both of their statements have fallen apart. I'll be damned. I think you've got something there, Chase."

She grinned. She had given the detective something useful. He would soon find out Julie did *not* kill anyone. "I have another question. Does Dickie Byrd's alibi stand up?"

"Do you know what his alibi is?"

"No, but if Mona says he was with her . . ."

"I always take a spouse's protection with a grain of salt."

"If Dickie wasn't home all night, was he with his mistress?" Quincy became more insistent with his head-butting.

"Why do you call him Dickie? Is that what most people call him?"

"Probably not, nowadays. It's a nickname from high school."

"Does he prefer it?"

"I don't think so. I'm pretty sure he dislikes it."

"Then why do you use it?"

That was a good question. Maybe she shouldn't. She had rarely called him anything else, but they weren't kids anymore. He didn't even remember her. "You're right. I should call him Richard." One more good bump from the cat and her phone flew to the floor.

She dumped Quincy off her lap and snatched up her phone. "Are you still there?" The battery had fallen out and was on the floor. She put it back together, but the detective didn't answer her call. She didn't know much more about Dickie's alibi now than before she called.

"You little dickens," she scolded, picking Quincy up and stroking his back. "You've had plenty of exercise. Why are you so feisty today?"

A sudden sneeze sent the cat to the floor and Chase grabbing a tissue from the box on her desk.

She abandoned her work on the inventory and took the cat upstairs so he could use up some of his energy batting a Go Go Ball around the apartment. It was her day off, after all, and she shouldn't be working. She'd only been doing it to occupy her mind, since she wasn't getting anywhere replacing Julie as the main murder suspect on Olson's list.

A gentle snowfall started. It was about three in the afternoon. Her throat felt a bit scratchy, so she made a cup of decaf English Breakfast tea and poured a generous amount of honey into it. She snuggled into the corner of her comfy chair, sipping her sweet home remedy, and watched the flakes, falling straight down in the absence of even a breath of wind.

At four, she jerked her head up, suddenly awake. The doze

had felt good. She was energized. But what had awakened her? Her doorbell sounded. That must have been what she had heard. Her cell phone signaled distress that the battery was low, too, so she plugged it in first.

She stepped into her slippers and ran down the stairs. When she opened the door, Professor Anderson Fear stood there fidgeting, his shoulders frosted with snow. His fat-tire bicycle leaned against the wall behind him, which meant that he had pedaled over in the snow.

"Ms. Oliver? Can I speak with you?" His pinched face showed worry.

"Of course. Come on in." As she spoke, she realized her throat didn't feel much better. She had caught Grace Pilsen's cold, curse the woman.

She led him up the stairs to her apartment and pointed him to the leather couch. It would be less affected than her chair by the snow that would melt off him. After taking off his coat and draping it over the arm, he sat. Quincy eyed him, but didn't jump up beside him. The cat very much disliked being wet.

Professor Fear's dark, disheveled hair was coated with white flakes as well. He took off his glasses and polished the thick lenses on the tail of his mud-brown sweater. "I'm worried about Hilda."

"Is she all right?" Chase also knew that her health wasn't excellent.

He drew a shaky breath. "Physically, yes. I'm not sure about her mind lately, though."

"What's happened?" Chase unwrapped a cough drop and popped it into her mouth.

"I went to check in on her this morning and a man was leaving her house. I'm certain he's the one who was there before. The man she said looked like an egret."

"Van Snelson, the high school principal."

"Yes, yes. She calls him Nelson, but that's the one. I ran right in and asked her what had happened."

"She did promise not to sign anything, right?"

"That's what she said." His hair had dripped melted snow onto his glasses. He took them off again and rubbed them against the sleeve of his sweater, then stuck them back on his nose. "That's what she agreed to then, when you were talking to her. But she said today the man had a paper she needed to sign immediately."

"She signed it?" Chase sat up straight, her eyes wide. "Did you see it?"

"Yes, she signed. And no, she doesn't have a copy."

"No copy. This is bad. I need to call Julie." Chase jumped up and almost tripped over Quincy, who was curled at Professor Fear's feet. Her cell phone was in the kitchen on the charger. She left it plugged in and stood beside the counter, since it probably didn't have much charge on it yet. Her body thrummed as she listened to Julie's phone ring and ring. And ring.

As soon as Chase broke the connection, Julie returned her call, much to her relief.

"Hi, I was on another call," she said. "It was Gerry."

"Gerrold Gustafson?" Julie's lawyer.

"Yes, he wants to meet me after work to go over some things."

"What does he think?" She stopped to sneeze.

"What was that?" Julie asked.

"I'm getting a cold." It came out sounding more like "I'm geddig a code." She continued. "Does he think they'll charge you with murder?"

"He doesn't really say. But I know he'll do everything he can. What did you call about?"

"Oh, Julie. This is bad. Hilda Bjorn signed a paper for Van Snelson. Professor Fear is here and he says Snelson was leaving this morning when he arrived and Hilda had just signed something."

"Well, what did she sign? A contract?"

Chase called to the man in the living room. "Did she say anything about what the paper was?"

"She has no idea," he said, coming into the kitchen. "But I've talked to some others on our block. Some have signed contracts with him and some are refusing. More have signed than not and they're mostly elderly. That man should be locked up. I think he was going to come to my house next, but he saw how angry I was that he was at Hilda's."

For the scheme to work for Snelson and Hail, they would have to acquire all the houses on the block. Chase wondered if they truly thought they could do that. "I wonder how he thinks he's going to get you and some of the others to sign," Chase said.

"Listen," Julie said. "I'll tell Gerry that I'll be a little late. I'll stop by Hilda's right after work and see if I can find out anything. Oh, I have an idea. Maybe he'll come there with me."

"It might be better if both of you showed up on Snelson's doorstep," Chase said. "You could double-team him and maybe frighten him enough to tear up whatever it was he tricked her into signing."

"That's an idea. I'll call Gerry back right now. And you should gargle some salt water."

"Call me and let me know what happens. Good luck."

Chase broke the connection and told Professor Fear that Julie and another lawyer were going to work on it. "They'll either talk to Hilda or to Snelson." A coughing fit overcame her.

"Or both, I hope. Thanks for your help. And thank your friend Julie, too. That's a nasty cough. You should take a hot, steamy shower."

"I'll thank her." Maybe she would try the shower, too. She followed him downstairs, locked the door, and trudged back up.

Quincy meowed to greet her, then dug a Go Go Ball out from under the stove and purred.

"You shouldn't hide things like that," Chase said to the cat. "You always forget where you put them. Speaking of hiding things, I wish I knew where my gloves are. I'll bet you hid them, too." She was getting tired of wearing the ones with holes in them. When she felt better, she would search her place for Quincy's hidey-holes.

TWENTY-FOUR

Maybe Professor Fear knew what he was talking about. It was worth a try. She spent the next hour, after a steamy shower that temporarily stopped her cough, blowing her nose and sucking cough drops. She was starting to get sick to her stomach from them. Oh well, he probably wasn't a professor of medicine. Come to think of it, she had no idea what his field was.

She took a moment to direct a few dark thoughts at Grace Pilsen. Why had that woman come into the shop and sneezed all over Chase like that last week? Anna had never liked her and Chase was fully on Anna's side with that now.

Julie had had a suggestion, so she would try it, too. She salted some water and tried gargling in the bathroom. Unfortunately, she swallowed some. After that, she had a hard time keeping it from coming back up, so she quickly gave up on that idea. Shuffling to the kitchen, she fixed another cup of tea with honey and retreated to her bed.

Before she fell asleep, though, Mike Ramos called. She dreaded answering it. How could she explain that she'd been walking with Eddie Heath today? The phone stopped ringing, but started up again a half minute later.

"Hi, Mike," she croaked. The remedies she had tried so far seemed to have moved the malady to her vocal chords.

"Are you sick, Chase?"

"Uh-huh."

"You sound awful."

Go ahead and say it, she thought. Tell me I shouldn't have been out walking with Eddie.

"I'll call again tomorrow. You should get plenty of rest tonight. Do you have a cough?"

"A bad one." She demonstrated for him, unwillingly, and almost couldn't quit.

"Sleep with an extra pillow or two. It helps your cough if you're not flat."

"'Kay, I will."

That had been easy. Maybe next time she didn't want to talk about something, she'd get a bad cold. It probably would help to prop up, as he had suggested, so she got two more pillows off her top closet shelf and bolstered herself. She sipped more tea and read several chapters of Kaye George's Neanderthal mystery *Death in the Time of Ice* with Quincy curled beside her, then nodded off.

A phone call from Julie awoke her two hours later. She groped for her phone and tried to say, "Hello."

"You sound worse," Julie said.

"I am," Chase managed to say.

"Just listen, then. Don't try to talk. Gerry has some good ideas for me." It was a relief to hear the lightness and hope in Julie's voice. "He says Ron North was killed in the parking lot and transported to where you and Quincy discovered him. He wants you to testify that I wasn't in the parking lot long enough for that. Other people from the reunion can back that up, too. He's talked to some of them.

"Now, about Hilda. We dropped in on her. She seems confused tonight. She says she signed something, but 'that nice man,' as she calls him, told her it wasn't anything formal. We tried to get hold of Snelson, but his wife says he's not home."

"She kicked him out," Chase whispered, finding that it was easier on her sore throat than speaking. "Detective Olson told me that."

"Great. That means I have no idea where to find him until school starts up again in January. A very good thing has happened at work. The other lawyers finally realize that I have nothing to do with the shady side of what those two are doing. I'm no longer getting dirty looks in the break room."

"I'm glad of that."

Chase hung up and immediately fell asleep again.

This time, when she woke up, she was disoriented. Two pillows loomed next to her in the bed, looking like a lumpy person at first. Then she remembered she had been propped up so she could breathe more easily. Her clock said it was already 10:00 PM.

Anna would probably be up at this hour. She usually watched the news at ten, then worked her way toward bed.

"Anna?" she said when the older woman picked up. "I don't think I can come to work tomorrow."

"You sound awful. Julie said you weren't feeling well."

"A code in my head." She sniffed, but didn't cough.

"Grace Pilsen gave it to you, I'm sure. What a horrible person she is! I hope she's still sick at the Batter Battle."

"No, you don't. She'll come anyway and infect everyone there." Chase was whispering again. If anything, her throat felt more raw than before.

"I wonder if she could be disqualified for making the judges sick. Don't worry about tomorrow. The way the snow is piling up, we probably won't get much business. Both Inger and Mallory are planning on showing up."

"That's good." *Thad's goot.* No, she shouldn't talk. Whispering was far better.

"What are you taking?"

"I've tried a few things. A hot shower, saltwater gargle, tea with honey. The tea feels best."

"I can't do it now, it's not quite done, but I'll bring something over tomorrow. Try to get some rest, Charity."

"Will do. Love you."

Anna signed off saying she loved Chase, too. Chase couldn't wait to see what the next remedy would be.

In the morning, her bedroom ceiling glowed with the sunlight reflecting off the snow outside. She struggled to the window to see how much had fallen overnight. At least another foot. There was a little over two feet on the ground, not a showstopper for Minneapolis, but enough to keep some people home.

She was itching to go out and find Van Snelson. Maybe

he hadn't killed Ron North, but he was cheating an old woman and that made her furious. Julie and Gerrold were the better people to handle that problem, she knew. But, with Julie busy following up on the greedy real estate swindlers, she wouldn't be trying to find ways to prove she was innocent of the murder, in case a judge or jury thought it didn't take that long to strangle Ron North. That was up to Chase. It was Wednesday and Julie's court date was Friday. A shot of panic ran through her and brought on a coughing fit. She reached for a cough drop as her cell phone rang. Eddie Heath again.

"You opening today?" he asked.

"Bar None is open, but I'm not working today."

"Hey, a day off. Want to do something fun?"

"No, Eddie, not a day off. A sick day. I have a cold."

"Now that you mention it, you do sound bad. I'm closing up. The plows have put all the snow in front of my shop and there's no parking on this block at all. I'll be over in a minute with something to make you right as rain."

He disconnected before she could dissuade him. She would groan if her throat didn't hurt so much. Here came another home remedy.

Her only hope was that Anna got to the Bar None before he did so Chase wouldn't have to go down the stairs and let him in. She wished she could call him back and tell him to set his remedy outside the door, but she couldn't bring herself to be quite that rude.

TWENTY-FIVE

Chase heard the door open downstairs. Anna, she thought, relieved. Then she heard two sets of footsteps coming up the stairs. Hoping it wasn't Anna and Eddie at the same time, since Anna disapproved of him, Chase went to her door and opened it. It was Anna and Eddie, of course. She smiled to hide her uneasiness. Much as she knew she shouldn't keep seeing Eddie, she also didn't want him to see her with her hair flat and her nose red.

"Hey, let me drop this off for you, Chase," he said. "Drink as much of it as you can. It'll make you better in no time." He shoved a thermos at her, gave a mock salute, and trounced down the stairs. It was something hot. More tea with honey would be good, but she somehow doubted that's what it held.

After he left, Anna bustled in to set her contribution on the stove. She turned on a burner and soon the delectable aroma of Anna's homemade chicken soup was filling the kitchen.

"What did your friend bring you?" Anna asked.

"I'm afraid to look."

"Why is that?"

"He's into natural health stuff. You know, vegan, green stuff to drink, tofu."

"Those can all be delicious if you do them right."

Chase perched on her kitchen stool at the counter. "Not as delicious as your chicken soup. You're an angel for making it. Did you do it after ten o'clock last night?"

Anna smiled. "No, Julie called me much earlier than that and told me you were sick. I wish I could have brought it last night, but it was still too hot to transport when we were talking."

"You were talking. I was whispering." Chase started coughing.

"And you should still be whispering. This will be warm soon. Go to your couch, or your bed if you wish, and I'll bring it as soon as it's ready."

"You're the best." Chase made her way to the couch. She realized she was still clutching the warm thermos that Eddie had sent. Maybe it was a good hot drink of something that would soothe her throat, even if it wasn't tea and honey. Cautiously, she unscrewed the top.

A horrible smell erupted from the innocent-looking vessel. "Ugh!" She screwed the top on securely.

"What is it?" Anna ran in to see what had prompted Chase's outburst. "What's wrong?"

"I don't know *what* it is." Chase held the thermos out and Anna took the top off, taking a cautious sniff.

"Apple cider vinegar, if my guess is right." Anna wasn't disgusted, but Chase didn't know why not.

"Vinegar? He thinks I should drink vinegar?"

"I'm sure it's mostly water, with some vinegar in it. Apple cider. It's quite healthy."

"Take it away." Chase pulled her feet up onto the couch and Quincy obliged her by lying on top of them to keep her warm.

She dozed and was pleasantly awakened in a few minutes by Anna bringing her a bowl of chicken soup goodness. Anna's soup was mostly broth, which she got from boiling a whole chicken with herbs. Chunks of light and dark meat floated in the liquid with some peas and thin carrot slices, adorned with slivers of transparent onion. Anna used rice instead of noodles, which made it easier to eat. Plain crackers rested on the plate beneath the bowl.

Chase sat up and dug in. After three spoonfuls, she croaked, "Heavenly."

"Glad you like it." Anna beamed. "What do you want to drink?"

"Just water, I think."

"Good idea." After Anna brought her a glass, she said she needed to head downstairs. It was time for Mallory and Inger to arrive.

Chase heard them pounding on the back door as Anna ran down the steps.

As the morning passed, Chase felt her sinuses clearing and the fog that she'd been enveloped in lifting. By noon she was beginning to think she could venture downstairs. She hadn't coughed for an hour. If she started again, she'd return to her apartment.

Quincy's paws tapped the treads behind her as she walked down and into the warm, bright kitchen. The smell of almond flavoring prevailed. "Mm." She closed her eyes and inhaled. "You're making Cherry Almond Oatmeal Bars, aren't you?"

"There you are. Feeling any better?"

"Your soup is a miracle cure."

"Do you need some more? I have more broth at home. I can whip up some more soup for tonight if you'd like."

"There's some left. Is there anything I can do? Do you need a taste tester?"

Anna laughed. "There's a batch cooling on the counter. Help yourself. But don't touch the bars we're going to sell. I don't want our customers to get sick."

"I probably shouldn't be in the kitchen at all." She ducked into the bathroom to bathe her hands in the antiseptic gel, then snatched a piece of cherry almond goodness. "Good choice for a winter day." She held the amazing blend of cherries and almond flavoring on her tongue as long as she could before swallowing. "The cherries taste like summer."

"That's exactly what I thought," said Inger, who had come into the kitchen for her lunch break while they were talking. "Are you feeling better?"

"Much. Anna made me her special chicken-soup cure."

"You know what I do when I have a cold?" Inger said. "I put some Vicks under my nose when I go to bed."

Chase nodded, but had no intention of trying that since she didn't have any Vicks. "I'll keep that in mind."

"Can you cover for me while I eat? Mallory is swamped right now and I'm starving."

Chase asked Anna, "Do you think I should?"

"You're not coughing and your nose isn't running. Make sure to sanitize your hands."

"I just did, but I'll do it again."

Both Chase and Anna knew that hands should be cleaned often in the salesroom. Not only for cold germs. Handling money was about the dirtiest thing a person could do.

Being more active was good for her, Chase thought, after she had lazed around yesterday and this morning. She felt so good, she had thoughts of bottling Anna's chicken soup and selling it in the shop as a cure for the common cold. She smiled at the thought as soon as it flitted through her mind.

"Who you laughing at?" said the customer in front of her.

Chase shook her head. "Sorry, I was thinking of something else. Are you ready to buy those?"

The woman looked familiar, but Chase couldn't place her. She was short, but voluptuous. Even beneath her heavy coat Chase could clearly detect her curves.

"Yep. Richard says these are his faves." She held out a box of Peanut Butter Fudge Bars and a twenty-dollar bill.

"Richard?" The woman sounded like Chase should know who that was.

"*Richard.* You talked to him yesterday."

Richard. Right. Dickie Byrd. This was the mistress. "Oh yes, you're . . . Richard's friend."

"I'm his squeeze. He's been spending nights with me since his witch of a wife threw him out last Saturday."

Chase took the money and counted out the change, scooping the coins first. "Last Saturday?" She felt like an echo machine. "Wasn't that just a few days ago?"

"If you call a week and a half a few days."

"So . . . Richard Byrd's wife kicked him out the Saturday of the reunion?" Bad night for marriages.

"Yep, that's the shindig that he was gonna take me to, then chickened out at the last minute and took her."

"You mean Monique, right?"

"I call her Moaning Mona, but that's the same person. He still doesn't know what she did with all his clothes. Why couldn't she dump 'em in the front yard like other wives do?"

This woman obviously had had some experience at breaking up marriages. She wondered if Monique and Mrs. Snelson attended the same class on getting rid of husbands, including their clothing. She wouldn't suggest he look in the dump.

"Here you go." Chase handed her the change. "Would you like another kind for yourself?" She felt something warm and fuzzy rub on her leg. She glanced down.

Quincy! She had forgotten to put him in the office. Maybe her head wasn't as clear as she thought it was.

It was lucky for the cat that no one had remembered to close him into the office. Enjoying the full range of the Bar None shop, he kept out of sight and meandered through the kitchen, finding delectable crumbs along the way. When

his main human went out to the salesroom, he slipped through the swinging doors behind her. Ever curious, he found a paper that had fallen to the floor and began to play with it, batting at it and extricating it from under the counter where it had lodged.

"What are you doing out here?" Chase said it more for effect than to ask a question. She knew full well that she hadn't secured him in the office when she came downstairs. Spending the morning dozing had thrown her out of her routine. She bent to scoop him up and a paper clung to his claw.

"Oh, there's Richard's poster. Aren't you supposed to have that in your window?"

"This *is* your Richard, isn't it?" Chase knew it was, but had to tack this down. If he had spent the night of the reunion with this woman, he couldn't have killed Ron North. Chase had been relying on him as a suspect.

"Of course."

"What time did he get in the night of the reunion?" Quincy squirmed in her arms after she unhooked the poster from him. She needed to get him out of the salesroom, but she also needed to be certain whether or not Dickie could have killed Ron.

"It was before midnight. Maybe around eleven thirty or so. He left the party and went home. Then he came to my place because he was locked out."

He probably wouldn't have had time enough to kill and

transport Ron. Chase wasn't even sure he could have lifted him into a car trunk. Dickie wasn't very strong. Chase gave up trying to indict Dickie Byrd, said thank you to his mistress, and went to lock Quincy in the office.

Were there any other suspects left besides her best friend?

TWENTY-SIX

When a fit of coughing took Chase by surprise, she turned away from the counter.

"You know what you need to do?" Mallory leaned in close to talk so the customers wouldn't hear. "Take a damp washcloth and heat it in the microwave for about minute, then put it on your face. It'll clear your sinuses right up."

"Thanks," Chase managed to say, although her cold seemed to be in her chest by now, not her sinuses. "Gotta go." She was horrified to think she might have infected Mallory, to say nothing of the customer she'd been waiting on.

Inger was done with lunch when she made it to the kitchen. Anna said she would relieve Mallory so the girl could eat. "But you go upstairs and rest," Anna told her. "I'll bring some more soup over right after we close."

Chase remembered her cat through her haze and took Quincy upstairs with her. She collapsed into her stuffed chair and sucked a cough drop until her fit subsided.

She was sick, for sure, but she felt worse about being discouraged that she couldn't find anyone to take Julie's place as the number one suspect for Ron North's murder.

Who else was there? The real estate crooks had seemed the most likely. Van Snelson, her former principal, for whom she had lost all respect, had spent the night at the high school. His actions were strange, but it didn't seem that he killed anyone. Completely separate from the murder and the real estate scam, how could he go to work every day and be in charge of teenagers when he couldn't stand them?

Langton Hail, the funny little vest-wearing guy, had been too drunk. Eddie Heath had seen him in his car the next morning, preparing to leave the parking lot hours after the reunion ended. She hoped that those two would be punished for bilking people like Hilda Bjorn, at least.

She admitted that Dickie Byrd had been a distant third choice. She wanted him to have killed Ron to avenge his wife's honor after she was accosted. But now the Byrds were on the outs. He probably wasn't interested in defending someone who had kicked him out. He hadn't spent the night with his wife, but with his mistress, the short, stacked woman who bought him Peanut Butter Fudge Bars.

Who else *was* there?

Wait! Maybe Dickie Byrd didn't want to avenge his wife's honor, but who said she couldn't avenge it herself? She was fuming mad at Ron, even threw her drink in his face.

Chase stumbled to the kitchen drawer where she had

stashed the copied pages of Ron's notebook. She spread them on the kitchen table and turned to the part that she and Julie assumed was about his serial stalking victims. J was Julie and M was Monique. He had been making the rounds of his old victims at the party. He'd tried Julie, had mashed his face into hers for a kiss. Jay had come to her rescue and nothing else had happened after that. No, Julie had *not* killed him.

But he had confronted Monique, too. She'd been piled on that night. First, her husband got stewed to the gills at his own campaign rally, which, Chase assumed, Monique had orchestrated exactly as she'd run all his campaigns in the past. He had ruined the night for himself and, most likely, for her. Then maybe Ron's attack was the last straw. She had left early, even slightly before her husband. She would have had plenty of time to kill Ron. Julie's scarf had been in Ron's pocket, so it was convenient for her to use as a weapon as her anger boiled over in the parking lot.

Maybe she started out merely accosting him, perhaps berating him. Ron was so annoying that things could easily escalate. Monique could get madder and madder. She would start yanking at her hair. Fire would come from her eyes. Her anger would overwhelm her and she would lose control and strangle him. As inebriated as he was, he wouldn't be able to put up much of a fight. Ron wasn't very large. If Monique were fueled by adrenaline and hatred, she could have gotten him into her car and driven him to the park while it was still dark. She could overcome her touching phobia in a blind rage, couldn't she?

"Yes," she said, pumping her fist into the air. Quincy

scampered away and jumped onto the couch. "Didn't mean to scare you, little guy. But I think I have this figured out."

She followed Quincy to the couch and dialed Detective Olson's number, but quit halfway through when another coughing fit overcame her. As she sucked yet another cough drop, she had second thoughts. What would she tell the detective? She had no evidence to support her conclusion. There were no clues. It was all supposition. If he searched her trunk he might find blood. Could she convince him to do that?

Maybe Monique would come into the shop again and she could ask her some questions. She tucked one foot underneath herself on the leather couch. Quincy sat in her lap and they both dozed.

Chase's head grew bigger and bigger. It started spinning, slowly at first. Then faster and faster. It whirled around, still gaining weight, sickening her stomach, spinning, spinning, spinning . . . until it exploded. She grunted as her skull flew apart and suspects came flying out. Snelson and Hail tumbled to the floor. Dickie Byrd flew out and stuck to the ceiling. Then Monique, yanking at her hair, spun through the air, staying suspended for an impossible amount of time. Chase grunted again.

Her lap was cold. Quincy had taken off when she had started stirring in her dream. She clutched her scalp, but it was intact. Her head hadn't exploded. She was going crazy with this cold and all these suspects who didn't kill Ron North. Quickly, before the details could evaporate, she reviewed everyone she had seen come flying out of her stuffy head, which did feel super heavy still. Snelson, Hail, and the two Byrds. No, no one new. Those were all the culprits. That was rotten luck, she thought. Why couldn't her subconscious have worked out the answer? Maybe it had. Monique was the last one out and she hadn't landed anywhere. The dream had been so vivid, Chase checked the ceiling, expecting Dickie Byrd to be stuck up there. She felt doom was barely beyond her sight, maybe down the hallway.

Her door opened. Anna let herself in with her key and arrived with more soup!

"I'm so glad to see you," Chase said. She breathed easier.

"You sound all stuffed up." Anna busied herself heating the soup. "I'll stay and have some with you, if you don't mind. We closed up a little early and I sent Inger and Mallory home. Did you know that Inger is moving into her apartment on Monday?"

"That's great. It will be so nice for her to finally get out of that house for good. Her parents are no treat."

"No kidding. Have you gotten some rest?"

"Yes, I woke up just before you got here."

"I'm glad I didn't wake you."

"You have to go to the police station with me. I had a weird dream."

Anna raised her eyebrows. "You had a dream, so I have to talk to the police with you? Are you running a fever?"

"No, I mean . . . those two aren't related. Well, only a little bit." She still felt slightly dizzy.

Anna put bowls and soup spoons on Chase's kitchen table.

Chase tried to explain her dream, but muddled it up.

The terrible impending-doom feeling she had awakened with was receding, thank goodness.

"So, Monique Byrd stayed in the air instead of on the ceiling—"

"Or the ground."

"—so she killed Ron North." Anna had a right to be skeptical when it was put like that.

"Really, though, I think my subconscious might have figured this out. She's the only person left with motive, the only one who hasn't been ruled out with an alibi."

"Tell me her motive again." Anna ladled her golden soup into the bowls and Chase inhaled the healing aroma.

"Ron was stalking her, so she killed him," Chase said.

"That's about all they have on Julie!"

"They also have the fact that Ron was about to expose the real estate swindle and he thought she was part of it."

"But that's just it. She's not," Anna said. "Julie has said her lawyer will point that out."

"What about all the cases where there's only one suspect, so that one gets the guilty verdict?"

"I don't know if there are all that many."

"There are some. And one is too many if it's Julie."

"I agree with that, but what can we do?" She gave a heavy sigh. "What are you going to say to the detective when you go to the station? After you infect him with your cold?"

Maybe she should. If he were sick, he might back off trying to get Julie charged. "I would like to point out that he should make sure Monique has an alibi. Then, when he finds that she doesn't, he should be smart enough to consider her as his new prime suspect."

"Eat your soup and get some rest. Call him tonight, or see what you think tomorrow."

"Tomorrow is Thursday! The hearing is—"

Anna's phone rang. She listened with a worried look on her face.

New information, thought Chase. They found something else that makes Julie look guilty. She knew it.

TWENTY-SEVEN

"I have to go," Anna said. "That was the florist. They can't get the light blue orchids I wanted and they'd like me to pick out some calla lilies to replace them."

Chase was relieved it was about the wedding.

Anna's wedding was mostly lavender and blue, with some bright lime-green accents. She and Julie had ordered matching lavender dresses, but they hadn't come in yet.

"I'd better go right now and see what they have. I don't want anything too bright."

Yes, Anna preferred muted pastels for everything to do with her wedding. Except the bridesmaid bouquets. Those were lime green. She wished the dresses would arrive and she could make sure they would be all right. If they never came, Anna would whip out her sewing machine and make them, and she didn't need to be doing that right now.

She hadn't seen Anna's dress. No one had. Anna was keeping it a secret from everyone, including her groom-to-be, Bill.

Anna finished her soup and whisked her bowl to the sink. "I'll check on you later tonight."

Probably to make sure I haven't gone to the police, Chase thought. But the wedding was a week from yesterday and the dresses weren't here yet. That was something she should work on. She called Julie.

"Have you heard anything about our dresses?"

"For the wedding? No. I've had my mind on a couple of other things. Can you check? I'm still at work. Gotta go."

Chase dragged herself downstairs to the computer to look up the order. Anna had assured them she would be able to do any alterations they might need. Better than actually making them, but was that fair? Having the bride alter her own bridesmaids' dresses? Fair or not, Anna wouldn't hear of letting anyone else touch them.

There was a customer service phone number listed on the website, but when she called it, a message said they had hours of eight to five Eastern time. It was five thirty and Central time, besides.

She sent an e-mail inquiring about the delivery date. There were no tracking numbers to trace where they were. She was getting a sinking feeling about the dresses. At least she and Julie had shoes. She'd been surprised when Julie told her she had bought Chase's for her and, amazingly enough, they fit perfectly. Better than any she had tried on. Julie knew her shoes. The dresses wouldn't have to match them since Julie had chosen a contrasting shade of dark blue. That and the bouquets were the exceptions to the "all pastel" rule Anna had laid down.

She trudged upstairs, probably puzzling Quincy, who wasn't used to going up so soon after he had come down. The soup sitting in her bowl on her kitchen table had cooled, but there was plenty left in the pan on the stove. She poured in the cold soup and heated it up. When it was warm, she ate it all, then fell asleep again on the couch.

When she awoke in the morning, she had a vague recollection of moving to her bed in the night. As her eyes opened, Quincy stood up and started complaining. Oops! She hadn't fed him his nighttime din dins. It was a wonder he hadn't awakened her during the wee hours. Maybe he'd tried but she had slept soundly.

After she hurried to the kitchen and fixed his morning meal, she stretched, realizing she felt good. That soup had revitalized her and finally knocked out the cold.

Then she realized it was Thursday! Julie's hearing was tomorrow! She had to draw attention to Monique Byrd today. She watched Quincy eat, puzzling out what to do. Monique didn't have a place of business, except maybe the vacant storefront she and Dickie rented for his campaign headquarters. It was doubtful his campaign would continue, now that they had split. Monique might or might not be home, but Chase didn't want to call to find out. Wherever she accosted the woman, she wanted to take her by surprise.

Ideally, Monique's car would be somewhere close and Chase would find an excuse to look into the trunk.

That's as far as her thinking had gone. How on earth could she come up with an excuse to at least peek into the trunk? Monique wouldn't let her, of course, because Ron North's blood would be there, but she wanted to hear her refuse to open it. That, to Chase, would be an indictment. More like a verdict.

She called Julie. "Do you have a sec?"

"I'm due for a short break in ten. I'll call you back."

When Julie called, Chase had eaten and was ready to lay out her latest conclusion. "Help me think of an excuse to look into Monique Byrd's trunk."

"Um, her car trunk?"

"Yep."

"Why do you want to do that?"

"To see if she'll refuse to let me."

"I'm sorry, girlfriend. You've totally lost me."

She was making it a habit to lose people lately. First Anna, now Julie. "I'm pretty sure she killed Ron North and that means there's blood in her trunk. So if she won't let me look at it, that means she killed him. His body was transported, right? It had to be in a trunk, right?"

"Some of what you said is logical, but what's that first part again? Why do you know she killed him?"

"She's the only suspect left who wanted to and doesn't have an alibi."

"Chase, I can't see her lifting a man's body into her trunk. She couldn't weigh more than one-twenty. Besides, he was strangled. How much blood would there be?"

"Okay, DNA. His DNA has to be there."

"She's not going to be afraid you'll find DNA with your naked eye."

Chase had to admit Julie was right. "Well then, how am I going to prove to Detective Olson that she killed him? As for lifting him, she would be full of adrenaline and he's not very big."

"He wasn't very big."

"That's what I said."

"No, you said he's not very big. Present tense. Anyway, I have to get to work. Love you."

Chase hung up, knowing that Julie suspected she was still sick and was raving feverishly. People were arriving below. She heard the door to the kitchen open and close twice. It was time she showed up for work.

In spite of what Julie must think, Chase felt much better this morning. She hummed "Climb Ev'ry Mountain" from *The Sound of Music* in the shower. She felt like that's what she needed to do, climb every last ever-lovin' mountain so she could clear Julie. In fact, she almost felt like she *could* climb one. It was so good not to be achy anymore. She was singing the words now, as she got dressed and racked her brain for a solution.

"Who's that tripping down the stairs so lightly?" Anna called when Chase showed up.

"You sound like the ogre talking to a Billy Goat Gruff." Chase laughed.

"Well, someone's in a good mood. Is that new boyfriend working out?"

Chase frowned. "He's not my boyfriend. Quit saying that. I'm having a hard time getting rid of him."

"Maybe you're not trying very hard?"

She shrugged. No, she sure wasn't. "Anna, what are we going to do about Julie? I know Monique should be in jail, but—"

Anna held a finger to her lips and Chase heard Monique's voice out front.

"A dozen of those new ones. The pumpkin ones."

"The Harvest Bars?" Mallory asked.

Chase and Anna stood silent, listening. Chase hoped a clue would drop. Anna, she was sure, was relieved Monique hadn't seemed to hear the fact that Chase wanted her in jail.

"And a couple of Peanut Butter Fudge Bars for your husband?"

It occurred to Chase that a lot of husbands like those. Even Ron liked—peanuts! There might be peanuts in Monique's trunk.

"Definitely not."

Chase couldn't stand it anymore. She grabbed some replacement boxes and pushed through the double doors, aiming for the round table nearest the kitchen. "Oh, hello, Monique. How nice to see you here." She hoped her wide eyes looked surprised.

Monique answered with a frown.

"I'm sorry. Is something the matter?" Chase was putting on the best innocent, helpful face she could.

Nothing. Only more frowning.

"By the way," Chase tried again, "the reunion was such

a good idea. I'm sure it was you who thought of having it. It's so terrible that tragedy had to ruin the wonderful memories of that night."

"It actually wasn't my idea. It was Dickie's."

"Ah. Well—"

"I told him it was stupid. No one has a fourteen-year reunion."

"It's too bad—"

"My idea was to invite the whole class to a fund-raising dinner. That way, we would know who his supporters were."

And raise funds, Chase added silently.

"And it wouldn't be limited to our high school graduating class, either," Monique said. "I have favors all around town I could have called in. I hated the thought of kicking off his campaign in a rinky-dink high school gym. I would have rented a hotel downtown, or the Minneapolis Club."

"You belong?" That was a swanky, exclusive place.

"No, but I know someone who does. He would gladly have arranged it. But no. Mr. Know-It-All Dickie Byrd had to hold a replay of the high school prom, complete with horrid punch and basketball hoops, with bleachers folded up at the sides."

"I agree about the punch, but—"

"Also complete, I might add, with the bad boys spiking it."

"There was one difference."

Monique shook her head. "Yes, we're all too old for that nonsense now."

Chase had been going to mention the murder in the parking lot. Monique's car sat at the curb in front. "Can I help you out with that?"

214

Monique held up her one box of dessert bars and raised her eyebrows.

"Oh. I thought you bought a lot more." No, she didn't think that, but she was desperately fishing for a way to get Monique to open her trunk. "You know, I think I have a flat tire."

"That's too bad." Monique moved toward the front door.

"You don't have a jack I could borrow, do you?"

"No idea. You're welcome to look. I have Triple-A. If I have a jack, I'll never use it."

Rats. She didn't have any objection. Or was she smart enough to figure out why Chase wanted to peek into her trunk and was trying to throw suspicion off herself?

"Could I? I'll be right out."

Chase ran into the kitchen and borrowed Anna's jacket off the hook by the rear door. "Be right back." She couldn't take the time to run upstairs for her own coat.

Monique was staring into her open trunk when Chase got out there. "What does a jack look like?" she asked.

"I think it's that thing over there." Chase pointed to the jack that was strapped to the sidewall. The trunk was tidy and clean. It looked brand new.

"Help yourself." Monique waved at the jack and set her purchase on the floor of the trunk.

Would she put food where she had transported a dead body? There was certainly no blood. No peanuts either, unless Monique had just removed them. Traces of peanuts wouldn't prove anything anyway, now that she thought about it. But, as Julie had pointed out, there could be piles of DNA that were undetectable with the human eye.

"You know"—Chase was thinking fast—"I don't think

this jack will fit my car." That might even be true. Monique drove a Toyota and Chase a Ford Fusion. "Thanks anyway." She put her hand on Monique's arm, knowing how she hated to be touched.

"You always were a little different." Monique jerked her arm back, brushed off her sleeve, got into her car, and drove away.

Chase made a face and repeated her words aloud. "You always were a little different." She decided to add something of her own. "And you were always nuts, Monique." As much as she hated to admit it, Monique acted entirely innocent. And that trunk was pristine. It was true that DNA would be invisible, but surely something would be amiss if a dead body had been transported in it. That carpeting looked like nothing heavier than a box of dessert bars had ever been set on it. She argued with herself that a good vacuuming would fluff up the fibers after Ron's slight form had crushed them. If he'd ever been there.

When she went inside, she wasn't needed in the sales-room, so she retreated to her office to think. Were any of the suspects on her own list ruled out completely? Were any of them even good possibilities? Were there any reasons for her not to lose hope?

TWENTY-EIGHT

C hase sat at her desk in front of her monitor. It displayed a
screen saver depicting a cat watching fish swim past. She
ignored the playful image and doodled on a pad of paper,
considering each suspect again for about the hundredth time.

Van Snelson. PRINCE in the blackmail book. Hated
kids, even though he had been a high school principal for eons.
Was getting into real estate, but not in a good way: swindling
poor Hilda Bjorn and others out of their homes. He had probably slept at the high school all night and not left the building
to murder anyone or stash any bodies. However, if he was
being blackmailed, he might want Ron North dead.

Langton Hail. PHOTO in the blackmail book. The partner in crime—no, more like the instigator of the real estate
swindle. However, he was an alcoholic, now trying to recover

by drinking vegetable-laden beverages at Eddie Heath's Health Bar. She shuddered. That night, though, he had been too drunk to drive and had stayed either inside the school or in his car until morning, when Eddie saw him leaving. If he was faking being drunk, he could have murdered Ron and returned, acting like he hadn't left. Not likely, but possible. Not only the blackmail, but having a newspaper article expose his dealings, was a fine motive.

Then there were both Byrds. At first she considered Dickie Byrd because he might want to defend his wife's honor from her stalker. When she found out they had split up, that motive had fallen apart. If Ron knew about the mistress, though, that could hurt his campaign, so that was a very good motive. He had spent the night with that mistress. She might have fallen asleep while he slipped out, murdered Ron, dumped him, and crept silently back into bed. Not likely, but also possible.

Monique Byrd. Should she still be under consideration? She surely wanted to get rid of the annoying man. Enough to murder him? Had he been in that trunk and not left a trace?

The scenarios were all possible, but not probable. The trouble was, none of the alibis seemed ironclad, while all of the motives were good.

That faint J penciled in below the other blackmail victims was probably Julie. It wasn't good that she appeared in both parts of Ron's notebook, the blackmail part and the stalking part.

Maybe it was time to review that night another time and go over every single thing she could remember.

She had arrived with Julie, who immediately found Jay.

Chase talked to Bart Fender at the punch bowl, then Julie and Jay came over. Jay soon left with some guys and Bart wandered off.

Then Ron North had approached the two women. Ron started talking about Julie being part of the real estate scam. He seemed at least half drunk, and offered to spike their drinks. Then he attacked Julie and kissed her. Jay pulled him off and he and Julie left Chase with Ron.

However, she left and joined a group of women from her English class and they chatted for a good while. She observed Ron, still at the punch bowl, with some classmates and Mr. Snelson. Mr. Hail was with him. The two older men both left angry, possibly after Snelson paid him blackmail money, and joined Dickie Byrd.

Then Ron accosted Monique Byrd when she got punch. She threw her punch in his face. Bart started over, probably to do harm to Ron, but Ron skedaddled out the door to the parking lot. Bart followed him.

Julie had been in the parking lot with them, unfortunately. Chase didn't notice her leave or return. She couldn't testify as to how long Julie had been missing. How could the other, unnamed classmates do that?

The next thing Chase remembered was being approached by Eddie Heath. People were beginning to leave.

Who else had been in the parking lot at about that time? Probably lots of people. How could someone have killed Ron North and not been seen?

Bart had followed him out immediately. If he worked quickly, he could have done it. He was strong enough to strangle skinny Ron North. Chase had detected flashes of rage from him and wondered if he had Roid Rage from the steroids he was most probably taking. But why would he kill Ron? For bothering Monique Byrd? For blackmailing two men, one of whom was his boss? For mashing Julie, with whom he had almost no interaction? It didn't seem that any of the letters in the notebook could mean Bart Fender. There were no Fs and the only B had to be Dickie Byrd.

Rats. Here was a good suspect with opportunity and means—and no motive.

The butterscotch tabby grew bored with nothing going on. She was sitting there, not even typing. When she worked on the keyboard, he often jumped into her lap, never mind that it made it doubly hard to type that way. It got him attention. Sometimes he even jumped onto the keyboard. That could be counted on to cause a lot of commotion. This writing on paper business, however, was extremely boring.

He decided to check on his stash. He snaked a claw under the desk and pulled the material out a bit. Yes, it was still there.

"My gloves!" Chase plopped down onto the floor. "There they are! You pushed my gloves under the desk, didn't you, you pesky cat." She fished one out, pushing Quincy away. He wanted to play with it, but she needed her good gloves. The weather was turning colder and colder and she didn't see any sense in buying a new pair when she already owned these.

"The other one is under here, too, isn't it?" she asked him. She knelt down, putting her head on the floor to see better. Something was under there, for sure. Reaching up to her desk drawer, she withdrew a wooden ruler and used it to get at the other glove.

"There! I'm so glad I found these." She picked them up. A piece of paper dropped to the floor. She retrieved it. Why did it look so familiar? It had been torn from a spiral note-book, judging from the shredding on one side. The paper was small and lined. She squinted to make out the faint pencil writing. It held some words in capital letters and amounts next to them. It was another page from Ron North's notebook!

TWENTY-NINE

C hase set the page on her desk, carefully, and called Julie. The cell phone rang over to voice mail.

"Call me," she barked. She glanced at the clock. Two in the afternoon. Julie was, no doubt, in the middle of something at work.

She got up and started pacing. The paper was yellow and brittle. It must have fallen out of the notebook when they first started examining it. Maybe it was a page from an older notebook that Ron had stuck into the newer one. The louse had been blackmailing people for a long time. It was a wonder he wasn't rich. Or hadn't been killed years ago.

Stopping long enough to peer at the paper, she bent close over the desk. Squint as she might, she couldn't quite make out the smudged writing. Was the first letter H? If she could find a way to connect this with another blackmail victim, even if it was an older one, there would be another suspect.

"Charity? Tanner is here," Anna said as she rapped on the office door.

Chase opened the office door, careful to keep Quincy contained. "Hi, Tanner. How's it going?"

"Hangin' in there. Do you have a check for me?"

"I was going to mail it tomorrow, but you can have it today." Since he'd come by, he must need the money. She wrote him a check, wishing she could pay him more. Maybe she would be able to some day. He deserved it, having done such a great job on the webpage. "I've heard people say they found our shop on the Internet, so the page is working."

"Great." His smile lit up his skinny face as he took his money. His nose and eyebrow rings glinted in the glow of the moving screen saver.

"What's this?" He reached for the page.

"No, don't touch it." Chase caught his hand. "It's old and pretty delicate. I just found it under my desk. I think the cat put it there."

"Why is it so special?"

"I think it's an old page from the notebook of the man who was murdered."

"That one I hacked into? That rnorth83 guy?"

"You remember his e-mail name?"

"Sure. He was emailing bigbyrd about some pictures he had."

"Do you want to look at this paper and tell me if you can decipher what it says?"

Tanner left it on the desk, but adjusted the desk lamp to

shine more brightly on it. "H something, right? HU? Should I go into his account again and see if he e-mailed anybody with HU in their name?"

"Can you do that? Do you have time?"

"No problem."

That was a good idea. "Have a seat," she said, waving him into her desk chair.

The cat and the fish disappeared and Tanner started working. His long, thin fingers flew over the keys, clicking so loudly that Quincy stared. Chase stared, too, hoping to see the name of the murderer displayed on the screen, along with a picture and personal statistics. That always happened for the sleuths on TV.

"You can go do something else while I work," he said.

She was probably making him nervous, hanging over his shoulder. "I'll be in the kitchen."

Anna had a batch of her favorites, Lemon Bars, coming out of the oven, so Chase grabbed a hot pad and slid the dessert bars onto a cooling rack. She picked one up with a paper towel and blew on it to cool it.

Mallory poked her head into the kitchen. "Did I hear Tanner come in?"

"He's in my office," Chase said. "He'll be out in a few minutes." Maybe.

Mallory's face split into a huge grin. "Okay. Tell him I'm here."

Chase assured her she would. She loved seeing this young love blossom before her eyes. Mallory was working hard at smiling at the customers, and she was doing a much better job than when she'd started working at the Bar None. But no customer had ever gotten the grin she had given at the thought of Tanner being near.

She popped the Lemon Bar into her mouth, closing her eyes as the sweet-tart flavor melted on her tongue.

In less than half an hour, Tanner emerged. "I got it. Wanna see?"

Chase hurried into the office. Tanner pointed to the screen. He had gotten into Ron North's e-mail account again.

"How long before someone shuts this down?" she asked.

"It might stay out there for years, unless the cops want to close it."

This time the messages were between rnorth83 and someone called hunkyb.

hunkyb: not tellin u agin

rnorth83: wotz ur problem man

hunkyb: its all yr fault stay away from her its all yr fault

rnorth83: or?

hunkyb: ill smash in ur ugly face

rnorth83: like u did last time

hunkyb: this time ill do it

"So," Chase said, trying to figure out what was going on in this exchange. "Hunkyb warns Ron to stay away from . . . someone, a female."

"Probably his girlfriend. Or wife. And looks like North was stalking her, like he did all those others. Is she in the notebook?"

"How would I tell?"

"Let's look at it again."

"Better yet," Chase said, "let's figure out who hunkyb is. This older page references someone beginning with H."

"Can I touch it? I'll be careful." Tanner pointed to the brittle paper.

Chase bit her lip, but nodded.

Tanner grasped the paper at the corner and held it up to Chase's desk lamp. The letters leapt into clarity, seen with the backlighting.

"HULK," they both said together.

"Great," Chase said. "Now we have to figure out who both HULK and hunkyb are."

"Probably the same person. North gave people nicknames. He wouldn't call the guy the same thing the guy called himself. This sounds like a big person, either name you use."

"Someone who thinks he's good looking, since he calls himself a hunk."

Her cell phone rang. It was Eddie Heath. A shiver ran up her spine. Eddie wasn't tall, but he was muscular. And his last name started with H.

THIRTY

"Aren't you going to answer that?" Tanner asked.

"I'd better. It's . . ." She couldn't explain in two seconds that Eddie Heath thought a lot of himself, had a lot of muscles, and had a name beginning with H.

"Eddie, it's good to hear from you."

Tanner raised his eyebrows. He had seen her reluctant, maybe scared face along with her hesitation and doubted her words, she was sure.

"Oh yeah? Why's that?" Eddie asked. Why did he do that? He hadn't seen her face.

"Just, you know. To thank you for the vinegar stuff." Yeah, right. She would never drink that in a million years.

"Hey, did my cure work? You sound a lot better."

"Yes, tons better." She pointed to her phone and then to the page with the H. Tanner nodded.

"Are you up for a walk?" Eddie asked.

"Not right now. The shop is open. Isn't yours?"

"I did open today, but I have help here. We got the parking spaces cleared again this morning. Got a lot of customers today, too. That little guy, Hail, he came in for his smoothie."

"That's nice."

Tanner was looking concerned. He scribbled something on a scrap of paper—not the one from the notebook, she was glad to see.

Ask for his e-mail address.

She nodded. "Eddie, could you do me a favor? Could you e-mail me the recipe for that vinegar cure?"

"I can make it for you whenever you want."

"I'd really like to have it, though. I'd like to . . . show it to some other people."

"Sure, if you want."

She gave him her e-mail address and he said, "I'll get to it later today. I'm not at the store now. So, a walk later?"

"I . . . I'd better not chance it. I'll wait until I'm one hundred percent healthy. I'm afraid I'll relapse." That much was true. "Thanks anyway."

"Sure thing. See you later."

"Well?" Tanner asked after she finished the call.

"He'll e-mail it 'later.'"

"Remind him if he doesn't do it today."

She thought that would be a very good idea. Then, when she was sure, she'd call Detective Olson with some real evidence and he'd have to investigate Eddie instead of Julie. Unless she could get a little more information from him. Dare she?

"Tanner, you're a gem," she said. She leaned over and kissed the top of his head.

"Aw. Thanks." His skin reddened on his neck and the flush rose to the tips of his ears.

"You'd better go tell Mallory you're here."

He rushed out of the office.

She picked up the copies of the notebook and turned to the section where Ron kept track of his stalking victims. Maybe there was a tie-in with HULK and the women. The ones listed first, which she presumed were older, were M and J. Monique and Julie, they had assumed, since he had harassed and terrified both of them in high school. Then there were the others: D, K, L, and the mysterious Q. They could be anyone.

Julie called and she put the papers down.

"Sorry I was busy before. Do you have any good news for me?"

"I might. I think a page fell out of that notebook we gave to the police. Quincy must have shoved it under my desk. It was there with my gloves."

"Your good gloves? You found them? Great."

"Yes, I'm happy to finally have them back. But this page is the real find. The paper is old, maybe from an older notebook. He lists someone he calls HULK."

"Do we know any large, green people?"

Chase laughed. "Tanner was here and he performed

another miracle. He hacked into Ron North's e-mail account again and found an angry exchange between him and someone beginning with H, hunkyb."

"Someone named B?"

"I thought it meant 'hunky bod' and this guy thinks a lot of himself."

"Could be. Or hunky boy, I guess."

"Julie, I'm afraid this might be Eddie Heath."

"Really? Eddie? Wow. If he's the killer that would be bad. Do the e-mails give a motive for murder?"

"They're angry and threatening. The hunk person mentions smashing in Ron's ugly face."

"Ouch. And you think this is Eddie? Are you going to stop dating him?"

"I'm not dating him!"

"Right. Are you going to stop seeing him? How long has it been since you've seen Mike?"

Too long. Much too long.

"Chase, we could use you out front," Anna called from the kitchen.

"I'd better get to work," Chase said to Julie.

"Me, too. Call me later."

The salesroom was humming with activity. It seemed that, all of a sudden, everyone in Dinkytown and beyond had decided that goodies from the Bar None would make excellent Christmas and Hanukkah gifts.

Chase looked up from counting change when she heard a familiar voice.

"Patrice," she said, "I haven't seen you in a while."

Patrice was next in line for Mallory. "I've been helping Mike out at the clinic. His assistant has the flu."

"That's terrible. So far all I've had is a cold." She rapped her knuckles on the wooden top of the display case for luck.

"I haven't seen you either. I asked Mike about that the other day."

Chase handed the change to her customer. "Thank you and have a nice day."

"What I mean is, are you and Mike seeing each other anymore?" Patrice went on.

Chase wasn't sure how to answer that. "We're not *not* seeing each other. It's, well . . . things are busy right now."

"He isn't that busy." She looked around the crowded shop. "I guess you are though, huh?"

"Yah, it'll let up after Christmas."

Patrice handed her box of Hula Bars to Mallory, who had taken about fifteen minutes telling Tanner good-bye in the kitchen, and who was now back at work. "Shall I tell him anything from you?"

"Sure. Say hi."

"You want him to call?"

"Sure." Yes, she did want him to call. "Tell him I'm thinking of him and would like to get together soon. I've been sick or I would have called before."

Patrice didn't seem convinced that Chase was sincere, but she left, promising to relay the message.

After the shop closed at 6 PM, and Mallory and Inger had both left, Chase helped Anna with the last of the cleanup.

"Anna, I need some advice."

Anna looked eager to give it. Chase knew that she liked
to keep track of Chase's life, and recently Chase hadn't been
quite honest with her about Eddie Heath. Anna hitched herself onto one of the stools and patted the other one. "Come
on. Sit here and tell me. This sounds serious."

"It's about Eddie Heath."

Anna nodded her wise-grandmother nod. "I thought it
might be."

How did she know everything like that? Patrice should
employ Anna when she did her fortune-telling act. "I don't
really want to keep seeing him. My mind tells me that, it
really does. But I end up with him whenever he calls. There's
such a . . . pull. It's like magnetism."

Anna nodded again. She patted the back of Chase's hand.
"Yes, it is. It's chemistry. And sometimes it happens with the
wrong people."

"What should I do about it?"

"You know the answer. Stop seeing Eddie." She squeezed
Chase's hand.

Chase slapped her other palm flat on the counter. "I will.
I'll do that. As soon as . . . I do have to touch base with him
once more. I need to know why he was being blackmailed by
Ron North."

"He was? Do you think he killed Ron?"

"Probably. I don't know. I would like him to be guilty
and for Julie to be in the clear."

"Then you don't see him again, you ninny. You give
your information to the detective."

"But I don't think there's enough to go on."

"Let the police decide. Don't you dare get close to that man again. Charity? You hear me?"

"I hear you," she said, but she didn't look at Anna when she said it and she knew Anna must have known she didn't mean it. She wouldn't see him alone, though. She would see him with Julie by her side.

"Meanwhile," Anna said, "you should take some dessert bars to Dr. Michael Ramos. He's gone without them for too long. Lemon, right? The same kind you like?"

"Right. I'll do that." This time she looked at Anna. "That's such a good idea. Maybe I'll take some over tonight."

"Wait a minute. Let me tell you about when this chemistry thing happened to me. Maybe you can learn something from it. When I was engaged to my husband, about a year before we got married, I met a guy at the roller rink. I first noticed him because of his fancy skating—crossovers and spins and even some hops—then I noticed how tall he was. And blond as he could be. Like a beacon in the dim roller rink.

"Well, he saw me watching him and gave me the sexiest wink you can imagine. I was a decent skater and I was skating along just fine, but took a tumble when he did that. He was right there to help me up and, I'll tell you, our hands touched and fireworks exploded right there inside the roller rink."

Chase could picture the young, graceful Anna on skates. She couldn't quite picture her going end over end, but she was getting a vision of the tall stranger.

"I didn't know a thing about him, but we went to the ice cream store for sundaes as soon as we could get our skates off. We met for lunch two, maybe three times, then he asked me out on a car date. Dinner and a movie, he said. Meanwhile, I was keeping all this from my fiancé and it was giving me stomachaches. I hadn't told my parents or anyone about him. But I fell asleep dreaming about him and woke up hoping I'd see him that day.

"We finally went out on a real date and I found out what a mistake I had made. Instead of dinner, he drove to a secluded parking lot out near Lake Minnetonka. I asked him what we were doing there and he said he wanted to talk and get to know me a little better. We had talked and talked at our lunches, but mostly about him. About how he was going to go to Harvard and probably would go into politics, or maybe law. He had, he said, graduated at the top of his class and the Ivy Leagues were fighting over him. To be sure, we hadn't talked about me much, so I agreed. But, deep down, I knew this wasn't right. I got that slight prickle you get when things are off.

"We only talked about me for a minute before he grabbed me and started kissing me. Even then, I didn't resist. He was a great kisser. But then, it seemed like there were four guys in the car, or one guy with eight arms. He was all over me, trying to get my clothes off."

"Anna! What did you do?"

"I pushed him away, but he kept coming. I started to panic, then I got out of the car and ran to the nearest house, which wasn't very close. Thank goodness he didn't follow me. I called my dad and he came to get me."

"Did you ever see him again?"

"No, and—it's funny—I don't even remember his name anymore."

Would Chase ever forget Eddie Heath's name? Of course, she was older now than Anna had been at the time of the skating masher. So probably not.

"Charity, I'm not saying this is the same situation, but I am saying you need to trust what your good sense is telling you and ignore the fireworks. They aren't reliable."

If only she could remember that when the fireworks were going off.

THIRTY-ONE

W hen Chase called Mike, Patrice answered the phone and told her he was doing emergency surgery and would be tied up for at least another hour. Chase decided she would surprise him. Would he be happy to see her? She wasn't sure. Should she go or not? Yes, she had to. But she was afraid she'd get a cold reception.

So she called Julie and arranged to pick her up and take her along. Strength in numbers. She needed a story. Maybe they would be passing by. With dessert bars? Okay, she would say they were on their way to dinner, but she'd been missing him and decided to stop in and touch base. Or something. That would be true if she talked Julie into dinner.

Chase hummed "We'll Meet Tomorrow" from *Titanic*

as she boxed up some fresh Lemon Bars. Not an entirely appropriate song, but that's what popped into her head.

Her cell trilled. It was Mike!

"Patrice says you called. So, what's on your mind?"

He sounded friendly. She was glad she had her story ready.

"Julie and I are going out to dinner and we had some left-over Lemon Bars"—that was a spur-of-the-moment embellishment, but a good one—"and I'd like to drop them off."

"Sure. I'll be here at least another hour waiting for this pup to wake up."

"What did he have?"

"Poor thing got hit by a car and his hind leg needed to be put back together."

Chase was glad Mike was the vet and not her. She didn't know if she could deal with the injuries he routinely handled. Poor little pup.

Chase sang "I Enjoy Being a Girl" from *Flower Drum Song* as she drove to pick up Julie.

Julie had readily agreed to grab a bite after they saw Mike.

"I've been working way too hard on a new real estate case. I'd love to take a break. So, tell me again, why did you ask me to come along?" she said.

"Things are tense between us right now and—"

"Well, duh. Quit seeing Eddie Heath. That might ease things up a bit."

"I know. I'm going to." As soon as she got one more piece of incriminating evidence against him.

Chase picked her up from work and she had a bulging briefcase with her. Julie had to drop off some documents to be signed at a real estate office near the University Medical Center. They discussed a few places to eat and ended up choosing a pizza place across the river, near the office Julie needed to visit.

"I don't care what I eat, as long as it's hot," Julie said.

"They have a Hawaiian pizza, loaded with pineapple and Canadian bacon. I love their cinnamon sugar dessert slices, too. The weather is perfect for it."

"Not perfect for much else, though, is it?"

The wind was picking up and the temperature had dropped rapidly as darkness fell. Small snow eddies swirled on the road, sparkling in Chase's headlights, and Julie reached to turn the heater up a notch.

The parking lot at Mike's Minnetonka Mills clinic was empty except for his pickup. Most of the shops were dark, but the lights shone from his window and door, the squares they made on the new snow warm and inviting. Chase hoped Mike would be as welcoming as those lights were.

He opened the door two seconds before they got to it. "Come in. It's getting nasty out there."

"Nastier, you mean," Julie said.

Mike smiled at both of them. "Where are you two off to?"

"We decided to get hot pizza on a cold night," Chase said.

"And didn't invite me?" He made a comical pouty face.

Was he kidding? Or did he expect to be included? Chase bit her lower lip.

"Hey, I'm only kidding," he said with an easy grin. "I

couldn't go anyway. The pup is starting to come around and his owner will be another half hour picking him up."

That was a relief. It would be fine to have Mike with them, but she felt they should patch things up before spending too much time together. It would be good to first get rid of Eddie completely, too. This wasn't nearly as awkward as she thought it might be so far, though, and that was a good sign.

"Patrice and I are going out later tonight," Mike said. "So don't worry about me. I won't starve."

"Is she doing okay?" Julie asked. She knew Patrice's history of filching things that didn't belong to her.

"I'm not sure. She said she had something to tell me, but I couldn't tell if it was something good or bad. I guess I'll see."

There was a lull and Chase searched for something to say. Mike raised his eyebrows at her. "Weren't you going to bring me something?"

"Oh. Yes. I left them in the car."

"I'll go," Julie said. "I forgot them, too."

"No, let me. I have to unlock the car." That was a stupid thing to say. Whoever went out would have to unlock the car, be it her or Julie. But she didn't look forward to being alone with Mike and another dead silence. She hated when that happened. The only two people that made conversational lulls comfortable, to her, were Anna and Julie. Maybe, someday, with Mike it would be that way. They had been on so few dates she could count them on one hand. If she saw more of him, maybe something more could develop.

She ran out the door. When she returned, they were gone. The room was empty.

"Back here," Mike called.

Chase went into the clinic, where the puppy was recuperating.

"Julie wanted to see Ruff."

A small dog stared at her with warm, friendly eyes. He was definitely a dog, but what kind? That was hard to tell.

"What is he?" she asked. "Some kind of . . . wienie dog mix?" Chase breathed in the smell of strong antiseptic. For some reason, she loved it.

"Hard to say. More likely one part corgi."

"With the coloring and fur of a Saint Bernard?" Julie asked.

"Seems that way, doesn't it? Ruff was a stray that was picked up and brought to the shelter. His owners adopted him from there. He's the friendliest little guy you'll ever meet when he's awake." He stroked the dog's black, tan, and white fur.

Ruff's long, plumed tail stirred and his tongue lolled out of his happy mouth. He couldn't stand up because of the splint on his left rear leg. Also because he was probably still too groggy.

"Good work, doc," Julie said. "He looks like he came through his surgery fine."

"He'll be okay once it heals. He's still young enough to mend quickly." He turned to the women. "Have a good time without me."

"We will," Julie said with a grin.

After they were in Chase's car, Julie said, "Cat got your tongue back there?"

Chase sighed. "I don't know what to say to him."

"I kind of thought he might ask you to lunch or dinner or something."

"I did, too." She would have accepted in a heartbeat. She wasn't opposed to women asking men out, but, for some reason, she wanted Mike to ask her.

"Maybe he assumes you're still seeing Eddie. You should clear that up, shouldn't you?"

Yes, she should.

THIRTY-TWO

After driving Julie to the real estate office that was staying open late for her, they drove to their dinner destination. Chase dropped Julie off in front of the pizza parlor and
went to find a parking place, since the small parking lot was
full. She began to worry if they would get seated inside an
hour—there were so many cars. After she finally found a
place around the corner on a side street, she got ready to
brave the elements. She pulled her knit hat down over her
hair and tucked her scarf more securely around her neck.
Before she could open the door, however, her phone pinged.

Hoping it was the e-mail from Eddie that would prove—
to her—that he was the killer, she fished it out of her purse
and opened the message. The subject was "Healing Vinegar"

and the text contained the recipe for the horrid concoction he had given her. The address the message came from was bhelthy. Be healthy? She cringed at the misspelling, then she threw the phone into her purse, discouraged that Eddie wasn't hunkyb.

She trotted through the snowfall, increasing by the minute, the sting of her disappointment worse than the nip of the cold on her face. Before she got to the front door, she had a thought. Eddie could still be hunkyb. She herself had two e-mail addresses. She had one that she gave to merchants to get them off her back, but she rarely looked at it. She had another main address she actually used.

If he did use hunkyb, though, he wasn't using it with her and she wasn't going to be able to use that as evidence against him. She had all the information she was going to get. Now, how would she relay this to Detective Olson? Tanner didn't want anyone knowing he had hacked Ron North's account. Could she tell the detective what was found without telling him who found it? She would have to think of a better way.

Before she went inside the warm restaurant, she called Eddie.

"Where are you, Chase? What's all that noise?"

"I guess it's the wind. I'm outside."

"Do you need some help?"

"No, I was wondering if you'd like to meet for a drink later tonight."

"You got some place in mind?"

They settled on Amble Inn, a place she'd been to with Mike once. It wasn't far from Julie's law office, where they'd left her car. Julie lived in that neighborhood, too, so she would drop her off and meet Eddie. And try to get something from him, anything. Some indication that he was being blackmailed by Ron, or that he was ever called Hunky or Hulk.

She would be very careful.

She and Julie were both surprised when Bart Fender came to the table to take their orders.

"You work here?" Julie asked.

"School coaches don't make as much money as lawyers." He smiled when he said it and Chase and Julie both smiled back. The order pad was small in his big paws. "Some of us have to work two or three jobs."

"Well, it's a nice place to work, isn't it?" Chase said, trying to soothe the fury that always seemed to simmer barely below Bart's surface.

"I don't know about that. But it's close to the hospital. I can visit Dillon before and after work pretty easy."

A pang of guilt stung Chase. For days, she hadn't thought of poor Dillon, lying in a coma, unaware of the battle that raged between Bart and her parents about turning off her life support.

"She's still there, then?" Julie said.

Chase wanted to kick her. She didn't think they should talk about this and rile Bart up. He'd been so upset when they'd seen him there.

"For now. What do you want to drink?" His smile had disappeared.

After he left, Chase whispered to Julie, "Don't talk about Dillon, okay? It upsets him."

"Yah, I can see that. I wasn't thinking. I won't mention her again. You're getting the Hawaiian, right?"

"And I suppose you'll have your usual pepperoni with extra cheese."

"I sure will."

"Listen," Chase said. "Eddie sent me a message, before I came in. It was from bhelthy." She spelled it for Julie.

"Is the guy illiterate? Or is he being cute?"

"Whatever. But the message wasn't from hunkyb."

"So we still don't know who that is and why Ron North was pestering him."

"Only," Chase said, "that hunkyb is likely to be the person who killed him."

Bart slammed their beers on the table so hard the foam splashed out on both of them, then took their orders with a fierce frown. Maybe it was hard to set things down gently with all those muscles. Or maybe they should both keep their mouths shut.

She whispered to Julie again after he left. "He's sure in a bad mood."

"Sure is," Julie agreed. "Let's eat fast and get out of here."

They ate and paid without incident and Chase dropped Julie at her office. Before Julie shut the car door, Chase said, "Wait."

Julie ducked her head back into the car. "Yes?"

Should she tell her she was meeting Eddie? This wasn't something she could do with Julie along. Julie would tell her not to do it, just in case he was a murderer. But they were meeting in a bar, one that was usually crowded at nine on a weeknight. No, she didn't want Julie to talk her out of it. Or worse, to tell Anna and have her get on Chase's case. The hearing was tomorrow. She had to do this.

"Nothing. I thought it looked like you left a glove on the seat."

Julie wiggled her fingers. "Nope. Got 'em on, see?"

"Call me tomorrow before . . . you know."

"If I can." Julie's teeth clamped on her lips and she left before she started crying.

How could Julie be so calm? She trusted her lawyer, but even so, if Chase had a hearing for criminal charges the next day, she would be fidgeting so bad she wouldn't be able to drive. She saw Julie get into her own car and start it up. They both beeped and Julie drove away.

Chase sat with her car idling, planning her strategy. She would try to get Eddie Heath to tell her all his e-mail addresses. Failing that, she would probe to see if he had any history that he could be blackmailed about. She worked out a strategy, or at least a way to approach this.

If none of that worked, she was going to alert the detective anyway. She called Niles Olson's cell number and it rang to voice mail. This was better than talking to him.

She spoke quickly. "I think I have a very good suspect. I'll know more in about an hour and will call you when I get home. Need to tack down some details. There's another page from Ron North's notebook to consider. Quincy hid it and I just found it."

There. She broke the connection, muted her phone, and headed toward the Amble Inn. She didn't want the detective calling while she was with Eddie.

THIRTY-THREE

Eddie frowned as he studied the bar menu. Now that Chase thought about it, she was surprised he'd agreed to meet her here. The Amble Inn wasn't a health-nut kind of place, simply a basic bar and grille.

"I don't find anything that's acceptable on this menu," he said, laying it on the table. "How can people eat like this? No wonder—"

"Sorry. I assumed you had already eaten. I thought we were having a drink."

"Oh sure, that'll be fine. You don't need to eat?"

"Just had . . . dinner . . . with Julie." She had been about to say pizza, but thought that might get her a long lecture. *How can people eat like this?*

Eddie picked up the beer list. "Did you know that beer has quite a few beneficial properties?"

"Really?" That's why he could meet her at a bar. Beer was good for you. As opposed to that toxic hard liquor, she supposed.

"It's actually just as healthy for you as wine. Contains polyphenols that are antioxidant. Reduces the chances of getting kidney stones, too."

"I was going to have wine, but I'd better have a brewski, then." Chase smiled. At least there was one consumable they could agree on. Two, with wine *and* beer.

Eddie cross-examined the waiter about what was on tap and ordered a raspberry ale.

"That sounds awfully good," Chase said. "I'll have the same."

"Peanuts and pretzels?" the waiter asked.

Chase said yes before Eddie could nix them.

"Peanuts are a good source of protein, but pretzels are pure salt and carbs," he said after the waiter left. She'd been pretty sure that was what he would say. Thanks to her jumping in, they would get the salt and carbs as well as the protein. Did the guy have to measure and evaluate everything?

To her horror, she recognized the trio getting out of the booth across the room. She turned her face and tried to shrink to nothingness, to become invisible. It didn't work.

"Chase! How nice to see you here." Patrice made her way between the tables with a huge grin.

Mike and Patrice's mother—Mike's Aunt Betsy—hung back near their booth. Chase couldn't look at Mike after that first glance.

"Say, I don't think I've apologized enough for making trouble for Anna," Patrice said, oblivious to the tension that stretched between Chase and Mike. She turned to Eddie. "Who's your friend? Have we met?"

"This is Eddie Heath." Chase tried for a smile, but her expression was probably too thin and tight to qualify. "He has a health bar not far away."

"How nice." Patrice shook Eddie's hand. Chase hoped he wouldn't be missing a watch or a ring later tonight. "See you around."

"Who was that?" Eddie asked after they had left. "Wasn't that the vet over there?"

"Yes, that's Dr. Ramos. Patrice is his cousin. I know her through him."

Eddie told a story about his first pet, a squirrel that had fallen from a tree. It hadn't worked out. As soon as the squirrel reached adulthood, it went crazy trying to claw its way out of the cage, until Eddie let it loose in his yard.

"I thought it would remember me and I could hand-feed it nuts after that, but it never came back. I couldn't tell it from any of the other squirrels."

After the beer mugs arrived—these served gracefully without sloshing, not at all the way Bart had done—she started in on her mission. She picked up the beer list, having noticed it gave her a great jumping-off point.

"See this?" She pointed to the verbiage at the bottom, asking the patrons if they wanted to be added to the mailing list. "Do you think anyone does that?"

Eddie shrugged. "No idea."

"I sometimes give my e-mail address to things like this,

but I use a different one. One that I reserve just for promotional stuff. In fact, I'm thinking of getting a third address for business. Do you have a separate e-mail for your business?"

"Nope. Only the one. I use it for everything. But I only give it to people I want to get e-mail from."

Dead end on that road. She took a swig of her ale. "Wow, this is good."

"That it is. I've never had it here. I'll have to remember it."

Her next topic would be anything Eddie had done that might be worthy of blackmail. Now how was she going to approach that?

"Are you going to want another beer?" he asked.

A kernel of a thought formed. "I think I'll stick with having only this one, since I had a beer earlier." Now she was going into new territory with him, making up lies. "I had a bad experience with drinking too much beer once. Years ago. Did some awfully dumb things."

"You have to be careful. A beer or two may be healthy, but being drunk isn't."

"Haven't you ever done anything you'd rather not have anyone know about?" She watched him carefully.

"Can't think of anything that bad."

"Anything that would get you, say, blackmailed?"

"Definitely not anything like that." He chuckled.

She didn't think he was lying. But his name was H and he was hunky and hulky. Was she totally wrong? Was she not going to be able to help Julie at all?

She must have looked defeated, because Eddie asked if something was wrong.

"No, but I have to get going soon."

"We just got here." He frowned. "Why did you ask me to meet anyway?"

She glanced up into the corner. "Oh, I wanted to see you. Touch base."

"Because it's been so long since you've seen me?" His sarcasm was understandable. She was making a mess of things now.

She thought of something he would believe. "I did want to see you, but I have a stomachache. Julie and I had pizza earlier and—"

"Pizza? Commercial pizza? That stuff is poison. No wonder you feel bad. Should I drive you home?"

"No, no. I'm sure I can make it. And I'd love to finish this delicious ale." That was true. She would have to come back another day and get a glass of raspberry ale she could drink in peace. With Mike, preferably, if he ever spoke to her again. "But I think I'd better go home and lie down."

"No, don't lie down. At least prop your head up. Do you have a recliner?"

She shook her head. "I can lie on the couch with a bunch of pillows."

"That would be the best thing for you."

She chattered while she fished for some bills from her purse. "People I know keep turning up tonight. I thought it was strange, but Bart Fender was working in the pizza place."

"Lots of high school teachers have second jobs. They don't get paid much." He reached across the table and put his hand on hers. The unwanted spark was still there. His touch went straight to her innards. She had a wild desire to grab both his hands, to kiss him, to . . .

"I'll get it," he said. "You go home and rest. Come by tomorrow and I'll give you something that will help if you don't feel better. It might take some time for that toxin to get out of your body."

"I have to work, but thanks. I'll probably be better soon."

She fled before he could offer to drop by with a health drink for her tonight.

THIRTY-FOUR

It was snowing hard when Chase came out of the Amble Inn. She trudged across the parking lot, horizontal crystals stinging her face. She shielded her face with her forearm, since she hadn't taken the time to wrap her scarf over her nose and cheeks. After she got inside her little Ford, though, and had caught her breath, she took the trouble to protect her face. She was going to have to get out and scrape her windows. After turning the ignition on and aiming the heat full blast at the windows, she got out and started scraping. Luckily, the new snow was a mere dusting, lying over a very thin layer of ice, so it all came off easily.

Back in the car, the inside had reached a toasty temperature. She dialed the heat down slightly and set out. It soon became apparent that the storm was just getting started. It worsened by the mile. As she drove through the almost whiteout conditions, she wished she had taken Eddie up on his offer to drive her home. She had driven through storms like this before, but had never liked it.

The traffic moved like a row of metal snails down the unplowed streets. There had been about two-and-a-half feet on the ground already and it might send them into record-setting territory. That was confirmed when she turned on the radio and heard the dire predictions. Maybe she wouldn't be working tomorrow, after all. If no one could get to the Bar None, workers or patrons, she could nestle upstairs with Quincy and stay warm and dry.

Once she made it home. If she made it home.

The car in front of her slewed as the brake lights flashed through the white haze. The rear end swung to the left. The driver didn't know how to correct the sliding and turned right, making the skid worse and spinning the car around.

Chase carefully applied her brakes, trying to stop before she hit it and also trying to avoid skidding herself.

The car kept spinning and swung into the oncoming lane where it clipped a truck. Both of them careened to the other side of the road, away from Chase's car with a sickening thunk of metal on metal. Those poor people, she thought, but was glad she was unscathed.

She pulled into an empty parking lot to recover from the fright. Taking several deep breaths, her mind wandered to everything that had happened that night.

Bart, working at the pizza place. He wasn't truculent at first. Had speaking about Dillon's coma upset him? Maybe. Or . . .

What had they been saying when he delivered their drinks? That's when he had started steaming. Panic iced the nape of Chase's neck, even though it was muffled in her warm scarf. They'd been talking about the e-mail, hunkyb.

Emergency vehicles, lights flashing and sirens wailing, sped past on their way to the accident she had just witnessed.

Chase squeezed her eyes shut and tried to recall the e-mail exchange.

rnorth83: wotz ur problem man

hunkyb: its all yr fault stay away from her its all yr fault

rnorth83: or?

hunkyb: ill smash in ur ugly face

"Stay away from her." Of course. It was Bart Fender. The D in Ron's notebook—that could be Dillon. She had been one of Ron North's stalking victims. Bart could very well have been threatening him. *What* was all Ron's fault? Dillon's coma? Julie had been driven nearly crazy by his harassment. At one point, Chase had been afraid she was desperate enough to hurt herself, but Julie had insisted she wasn't. Did Dillon try suicide because of Ron North?

If Bart were hunkyb and if he had killed Ron North, and if he had overheard them trying to put everything together, she and Julie may be in trouble.

She called Julie. "Did you make it home?"

"Just walked in. How about you?"

"I would be home by now, but someone spun out and caused an accident in front of me. I pulled over to catch my breath. I'm going home right now."

She told Julie what she had put together and told her to be very careful.

"You, too!" Julie said. "I'll keep my doors locked. Do you think he might try something tonight?"

"It's getting harder and harder to get around. I don't think so."

"Call me as soon as you make it home."

"I'm only about six blocks away."

"I don't care," Julie insisted. "Call me."

Chase promised to do that. She left her phone muted so she wouldn't have any distractions. Driving in this blizzard would take all her attention.

Her hands tightened on the steering wheel and her shoulders tensed as she pulled onto the treacherous street. She was unaware that she was speaking aloud until she heard mumbled prayers spilling out of her mouth. Her prayers didn't affect the snow, sadly. In fact, the intensity increased and the wind picked up in those last few blocks. She drove about five miles per hour.

By the time she steered into her parking lot, her whole body was as taut as a brittle gingerbread snap.

An older, beat-up car was the only other one in the lot. She didn't recognize it. Maybe someone had left it there and gotten a ride. Nothing was open on the block and hers was the only residence.

She glided to a slow stop near her door, got out, and locked the car door.

Again, she shielded her face with her right forearm, not bothering to pull up her scarf for such a short distance, and waded through the snow. It had drifted to depths of at least four feet in places.

It was hard to see even a few feet ahead. Her boot sunk into a drift and cold snow came in at the top.

After six or seven steps, an arm snaked around her neck. Instinctively, she left her right hand on her face, keeping her arm between her neck and the incredibly strong person trying to get her in a strangle hold.

"You're coming with me."

She smelled pizza sauce on his breath. It was Bart.

THIRTY-FIVE

There was no time to panic. She had to stay alive. First she tried screaming.

"Shut up." His voice was soft and menacing. "There's nobody to hear you."

"You let me go, Bart Fender! What do you think you're doing? I haven't done anything to you."

She tried to step back onto his toes, but he must have been wearing steel-toed boots. So she tried to kick higher, aiming her heel for his family jewels. He was too tall.

"You figured out I killed that weasel, Ron North. I can't have you telling anyone else."

Think, she told herself, think!

"After you pass out, you know what I'm gonna do with you?"

She couldn't bite his arm. Couldn't reach it. Anyway, they were both wearing bulky, warm clothing. And gloves. She began trying to shake the glove off her left hand.

"Let me go," she kept screaming. "Let go of me!" At least he wasn't cutting off her wind and she could breathe fairly well. Although he was pressing so hard on the left side of her neck that she was starting to see stars. She drove behind her with her left elbow as hard as she could and met with a solid mass of hard muscle.

He raised his voice a bit. "I said be quiet. You're annoying me. North deserved to die. He's the one who killed Dillon. He drove her around the bend. She couldn't stand to be alive anymore, even with me by her side. It's all his fault she committed suicide."

"She's still alive, Bart."

"Not for long. Everyone says she's brain damaged, she won't ever recover. She would be all right if they would be patient and wait, but they're gonna pull the plug and then she'll be . . . gone . . . forever."

She shook back and forth, trying to send them both tumbling onto the icy pavement that lay beneath the snow.

"Okay," she yelled as loudly as she could. "Tell me what you're going to do." Dare she hope that someone was within range to hear them? "You can't kill me. Other people know everything I know and—"

"Yeah, your friend Julie. She'll be next."

"Next for what?" she screamed, lunging sideways with as much force as she could, trying to dislodge the solid Bart, who must outweigh her by at least a hundred pounds, she thought. Maybe two hundred. How could she get him off his feet? She kept rubbing her gloved hand on her stomach, trying to dislodge the glove.

Tires crunched on the ice. Was a car coming? She couldn't tell if it was in the parking lot or passing by, out on the street, and she certainly couldn't look around for it from her position.

"I'm gonna put you under the same bush where I put North. Can't stand meddlers!" Now he was shouting, too.

Her glove fell to the ground. At last. She reached behind her and scratched.

Bart yowled, but kept his grip.

She reached again. This time she got an eye. She dug in and he let go.

Bart fell to his knees. Chase heard them crack on the icy pavement.

With one last, desperate lunge, he reached up and ripped her scarf off her neck.

She knew he wanted to strangle her with it. She shoved, pushed him over, kicked his head, and ran.

When she reached her door, she knew she would have to stop and unlock it. But when she glanced back, she saw a welcome sight.

"You're under arrest for the murder of Ronald North," Detective Olson said in his steeliest tone as he snapped handcuffs onto Bart's hands behind his back. "You have the right to remain silent."

"My eye! I need a hospital," Bart whined.

Olson ignored him and kept speaking. The rest of the Miranda warning was music to Chase's ears and she wanted to kiss Niles Olson on the lips right there.

"We'll have the doc at lockup look you over," Detective Olson said, shoving Bart into the rear seat of his car.

The ride to the station in the front seat of the policeman's car was warm, but they had to endure a constant barrage from Bart in the backseat. After Detective Olson called a couple of people, including someone about Bart's injured eye, he told someone else to impound Bart's car, then he turned to her.

"When you said you were onto another suspect, I got pretty worried about you," Niles said. "I had no idea where you were and you weren't answering your cell phone."

Maybe she shouldn't have turned the sound off. "The suspect I thought I was after wasn't Bart. The guy I questioned, I mean talked to, is harmless. Unless you're harmed by health food and too much exercise."

As they drove, the storm started to let up. The flakes slowed to a few dozen at a time and they fell straight down. The wind had vanished.

"We've been keeping an eye on Fender for a few months," said the detective. "So when I followed him to your place, it raised about a dozen red flags."

"A few months? What for?"

"I'm sure the chief will make a public statement now that he's in custody. I'm ninety-nine percent certain we'll find what we need to nail him for both crimes in his trunk tonight."

"For Ron's murder?"

"Yes."

"And?"

"He's been selling steroids to his high school athletes. We

were able to get three of them to flip two days ago. Before his shift at the pizza place, he picked up a new shipment. I was going to try to catch him in the act of distribution, but now we have him for murder. I'm sure North's DNA will be in his car somewhere. I heard Fender mention putting him under the bush just now."

Bart was howling so loudly behind them that Chase was certain he couldn't hear anything they said.

"So Julie is free. Right?" She cut her eyes sideways.

His smile made the warm car even warmer. "Right. Chief is getting hold of the judge. Someone will call her and her lawyer and let them know the charges will be dropped in the morning."

She slumped in the seat, suddenly so limp she could barely hold up her head.

THIRTY-SIX

When Chase finally got home that night and switched her phone on, she noticed that Julie had called. She had been required to turn her cell off while she was in the station giving her statement. Chase was tired down to the very middle of her melting bones, but she perked up when she realized she could give Julie the news.

"Jules! I just got home from the police station."

"Oh no. Are you okay? What happened?"

"It's a bit involved, but the end result is that Detective Olson arrested Bart Fender for the murder of Ron North and your case will be dismissed tomorrow."

Chase had to hold the phone away from her ear when Julie

whooped. Chase giggled with glee. How fun that no one else had told her yet and she got to break the news!

"I have to call Anna," Julie said. "If only it wasn't so late. I feel like celebrating and the roads are so bad."

"Let's do that tomorrow night."

"Do you think Anna will feel like it? Her baking contest is the next day."

"Sure." Quincy jumped into Chase's lap and his warm body felt heavenly after the cold police station. "She'll need a distraction, don't you think?"

"Maybe." Julie sounded doubtful. "We can try, anyway."

"Or maybe we should celebrate Saturday night. A double occasion. You getting off the hook and Anna winning the Batter Battle."

"Oh, I hope she does. You think she will? I'm crossing my fingers for her," Julie said. "I'll come by your place tomorrow night at any rate. What time?"

"Anna was thinking of closing up early and getting ready for Saturday, but Mallory and Inger both said they would stay to work. I think Mallory is going out with Tanner later. So, I'm free early. Are you?"

"I took tomorrow off, not knowing how long I'd be in court." Chase could hear a smile of relief in her voice.

Thinking of Bart brought the vision of Dillon, lying still and pale in her hospital bed, to Chase. "Maybe we could drop by the hospital and peek in on Dillon."

"Excellent idea. Two? Two thirty?"

"Three. I'll pick you up."

Friday afternoon, Chase and Julie made their way slowly down the hospital corridor. They were both reluctant to complete their errand, even though they knew it was something they should do.

"At least Bart won't be there," Julie said.

"Why not?" said a man's voice behind them.

Dillon's father was on his way to the room with two cups of coffee.

"You haven't heard the news?" Chase asked.

"We haven't left Dillon's side all day."

Chase was extremely relieved Dillon's parents hadn't turned off her life support yet.

"Bart Fender was arrested for murder," Julie said.

The man jiggled the cups and sloshed a bit of coffee onto the floor. A huge grin broke out on his fleshy face. It was transformed from the mask of sorrow, which was all Chase had ever seen, into a picture of joy. "Come on into the room. You need to tell my wife. We've talked about how unstable he was, so many times, trying to get Dillon away from him."

Both parents were relieved to hear that Bart was out of the way.

"Never did really like him," said Mrs. Yardley.

"We have some terrific news of our own," Dillon's father said after a sip of his coffee. "It's so nice you came by. This is a good time."

"Yes!" Her mother's eyes sparkled. "Dillon's brainwave has been picking up."

Chase and Julie couldn't help but notice the machines beside her bed. One showed a squiggly line that spiked a bit now and then.

Mrs. Yardley started to hum. Chase recognized the tune. "'Happy Talk'?" she asked.

"Would you mind?" Mrs. Yardley said. "I'd like to sing it to her."

"You can sing along if you'd like," Mr. Yardley said. "I do sometimes."

"She played Bloody Mary in the summer theater production of *South Pacific* a few years ago and she loves the song 'Happy Talk.'"

"Of course," Chase said.

Mrs. Yardley started and Chase joined in, when she could remember the words. There were a lot of them. Mr. Yardley hummed along and Julie was the spectator.

Chase wondered what the nurses and orderlies in the corridor thought.

"Wait! No, keep going," Julie shouted. More softly, she added, "See? Her brain waves."

The line was getting ziggier. Chase and Dillon's mother kept singing. Mrs. Yardley tightened her grip on her daughter's hand and Mr. Yardley had the other one. After two verses, Dillon's eyelids fluttered.

Everyone in the room held their breath.

Dillon's eyes closed again.

A nurse rushed in. "We have new activity." She seemed excited, too.

Chase gaped when she saw the line on the EEG machine jumping up and down, bouncing like a manic yo-yo. She blinked to keep her tears from falling.

Dillon's eyes opened again, found her mother's face, and her lips moved. She mouthed the word "Mom," then gazed slowly around the room.

The nurse looked at Chase and Julie apologetically. "I'll

have to ask you to leave. We've called the doctor. We'll need to do an assessment."

"Good luck," the two women called to Dillon's parents as they walked out the door. Two white-coated doctors rushed in a few seconds later.

Chase and Julie high-fived and left for Anna's.

THIRTY-SEVEN

Anna did indeed want to get her mind off the coming Minny Batter Battle, Julie told Chase, but she wanted to do it her own way. She had cooked up a huge pot of savory beef stew for the three of them.

Chase always loved being at Anna's little white house with the pastel blue shutters on Nokomis Avenue. Today, even more so, as the smells of hearty stew and baking bread drifted from the kitchen to the living room when she stepped into the house. She and Julie sipped a rosé. It wasn't Chase's favorite kind of wine, but Anna loved it.

They tried to help in the kitchen, but Anna made them sit in the living room while she finished setting the kitchen table.

"Okay, soup's on," Anna called.

"Stew's on, you mean," Julie said.

Anna stood ladling it out into thick crockery bowls as they took their seats at the small round table. The pale yellow bowls, with their plates beneath, sat on green-and-yellow-checked placemats. Fat carrots and potatoes, onions and cabbage floated in the thick, brown stew.

Anna wore a vest of vermilion and chartreuse over a yellow long-sleeved T-shirt. She stood out like a beacon against the pale mint green walls of her kitchen.

When they told Anna about Dillon Yardley waking up, Anna got tears in her eyes, and so did Chase—again. Anna was less pleased about Chase going off with Eddie Heath when she thought he might be a killer, and was downright upset about Bart Fender attacking her outside her own home.

"Grandma," Julie said, "it's all turned out all right. The detective took him in and a killer is locked up, awaiting trial."

"Is there any way he'll be found not guilty?" Anna asked.

"I suppose anything can happen," Julie said. "But it would be very unlikely. There will be traces left from Ron's body in his car. Juries love DNA."

"I hope baking juries love blueberry muffins," Anna said, worry creasing her brow.

Julie and Chase looked at each other. That was the subject they were trying to avoid.

"Isn't that courtroom drama on tonight? The one you like so much?" Julie asked.

Anna frowned at her granddaughter. "You're trying to distract me; don't think I can't tell." She softened her words and patted Julie's hand. "And I appreciate it. But I don't think anything is going to get my mind off the battle. I won't feel better until tomorrow night when this is all over."

"I almost forgot to tell you," Chase said. "It flew out of my mind. Right before I left Bar None to get Julie, Mallory told me that Grace Pilsen was in earlier."

"She came to our shop *today*? The gall of that woman!" Anna huffed.

"Mallory said she didn't look well. She was flushed and sweating and her eyes were red. She only stayed a moment. As soon as she was in the door, she started having a coughing fit and had to turn around and leave."

"She's sick again?" Julie said. "Maybe she won't show up to compete."

"Maybe," Anna said, trying not to smile. "One can hope."

Anna made hot cocoa and they sipped it, watching the tense drama unfold. The television show distracted Anna to some extent, Chase thought. She knew Anna wouldn't sleep much, but there was nothing she could do about that.

In the morning, the sun broke through the clouds that had covered the city for days. Chase and Julie, plus Bill and Jay, were all going as spectators. Bill drove Anna and helped carry in her supplies. Chase would have asked Mike, but she knew he was working at his clinic today.

The Minny Batter Battle was being held in the gymnasium at Hammond High School. Chase experienced a shiver of fear when she first entered the vast room. But gone were the long table and punch bowl, the banners declaring Richard Byrd as a candidate for mayor, and the rest of the reunion trappings. In their place were ten workstations, lined up in a neat row, as they were every year, according to Julie's whispers. From seeing other baking competitions on television, the setting seemed familiar to Chase.

From the bleachers, which had been set up on one side of the gym, Chase saw Bill stashing Anna's ingredients in the cupboard under the counter. Everyone had the same standard equipment: mixer, bowls, utensils, measuring spoons and cups, and baking pans, which were out and ready for use. Each baker was required to bring her own ingredients. *His* own ingredients in the case of the only man competing.

The room sizzled with energy. The stands buzzed with conversation as the crowds found seats, their footsteps drumming with a hollow sound on the aluminum treads of the risers.

Anna was chatting amiably with the woman to her right, appearing completely at ease. Neither one was actually at ease, Chase was sure. She looked for Grace Pilsen, but didn't see her. Eight of the workstations were occupied. The two to Anna's left were empty.

As the contestants got their things stashed, they then sat on the folding chairs provided. Chase knew they would sit there only until the starting buzzer, then would be standing and working for the rest of the time, maybe sitting while their concoctions baked, if they were caught up with all the other prep work.

A man with a handheld microphone introduced the five judges. One was a food columnist for the local paper, two were local restaurant owners. Chase and Julie quit listening and speculated on where Grace Pilsen could be and if she would show up. One of the places to Anna's left was no doubt hers.

A red-faced woman rushed in, her arms full of grocery bags, the coattails of her open coat flying behind her, and quickly settled herself on Anna's left. She peeled off her coat and plopped into the chair, breathing hard. But the station next to hers, the one on the end, remained empty. There were numbers on each station rather than names, but Chase was sure the empty place was Grace's. Where was she? Chase glanced at the wire-caged clock. Five minutes remained before the contest was to start.

A horrid vision rose, unbeckoned, in Chase's mind. She pictured Ron North lying in the parking lot outside at night. Then she pictured Grace in the same position. She had an urge to run outside to check it out, but couldn't leave when the Batter Battle was starting up in—she threw another glance at the clock on the wall—two minutes.

THIRTY-EIGHT

When thirty seconds remained until starting time, with all nine bakers perched on the edges of their chairs, ready to spring up and swing into action, in rushed Grace Pilsen. The white streak in her coal black hair waved as she sprinted across the room and skidded to a stop at her station. She shoved her materials into the cupboard, shrugged off her coat onto the floor, and, as her bottom touched her seat, the buzzer sounded.

All the bakers leapt up and extracted their bags and bins, clattering the equipment, intense concentration on each face, hands flying to put their concoctions together as quickly and flawlessly as possible. Judges strolled up and down the row, taking notes on electronic pads, their faces giving away nothing.

All the bakers except Grace. She pushed herself up and proceeded slowly, her hands limp and her face haggard.

"So she came. Even though she's obviously still sick," Julie said.

"I think you're right," Chase said. "I've never seen her look that bad."

"At least she's not next to Anna," Bill said. "But that poor woman beside her might catch whatever it is that she has."

As he finished his sentence, Grace reached into her apron pocket and stuck a wrinkled tissue to her face, letting out a mighty sneeze.

That caught the attention of the judge nearest her, a woman in an old-fashioned pantsuit. Chase wondered if it was polyester. The woman turned and stalked to the end of the row.

"That's Mrs. Prebbles, isn't it?" Julie said.

Realization dawned and Chase nodded. Mrs. Prebbles had been their home economics teacher in junior high school.

"She might be wearing one of the same pantsuits she wore to our classes," Julie whispered.

Chase tried not to giggle.

The other judges swiveled their heads toward Mrs. Prebbles and Grace Pilsen and watched.

Mrs. Prebbles reached Grace and began talking softly to her.

Grace shook her head and threw out her hand. Unfortunately, that was the hand that held her used tissue. The tissue flew to the floor at the feet of Mrs. Prebbles, who grimaced and stepped back.

A conference ensued, with all five judges and the announcer huddled a safe distance away from Grace. While they talked, Grace appeared to be stifling more sneezes, a forefinger placed delicately to her nostrils, and groping in her purse with the other hand for more tissues.

Meanwhile, Anna had gotten all her ingredients into her bowl and started the mixer. She scraped the sides of the bowl as it turned and took quick glances to her left.

The judges still huddled, some gesturing, others shaking their heads.

Grace fumbled with her bin of flour, trying to scoop some into her bowl but slopping a lot of it onto the floor. Even from where Chase sat, her trembling hands were obvious.

Chase looked down the line at the other contestants. Grace would be easy to beat today, even if she wasn't disqualified when the judges came to their decision. But were any of the others a threat?

The woman who had come late, right before Grace, was rattled. Not as badly as Grace, but she had managed to drop two of the three lemons she was attempting to squeeze. Julie whispered to Chase that if something hit the floor, you weren't allowed to use it. Anyway, Chase thought, that would be gross, even if it wasn't a rule.

The others worked competently, concentrating on their own projects, some of them apparently unaware of the drama at the end of the row. The lone man, at the other end of the row, looked the most professional—after Anna.

"Who is that?" Chase asked Julie, nodding toward the male baker.

Julie shrugged.

"That's Andy Pluck," Bill said. "He has an all-night diner a block from my pet shop."

"Are his baked things good?" Julie asked.

"I wouldn't compare them to anything at Bar None. He does a lot of cookies and pies."

"I've eaten there," Jay said. "His cookies are good, all very sweet, but his pie crusts are kind of thick and hard. Good fillings, though."

Chase surveyed the others. Maybe she was biased, but Anna was definitely the most professional. She got her dessert bars into the oven before anyone else. The contest was timed, so working quickly got them points for efficiency. Surely Anna had won that part.

The huddle finally broke up and the man who had held the microphone, now carrying a clipboard and pen, approached Grace.

Grace had managed to get flour, sugar, and eggs into her bowl and was starting to mix them together. The man motioned for her to stop. She looked up and frowned at him, the lines in her face making her seem even more haggard and much older than she was.

He was obviously asking her to leave. That must have been hard for him to do, since she had been such a big part of this event from its beginning. It was probably why the conference had taken so long. Some of them, if not all of them, must have been in favor of letting Grace compete.

When it came down to it, though, the judges would have to sample what each person made. Those who sampled Grace's products would be exposing themselves to whatever bug she was carrying. For Chase, disqualifying her would have been an easy decision, but she hadn't worked with Grace on the Minny Batter Battle like those people had.

Grace stood there stunned for a few moments, her eyes staring and her mouth hanging open. Then she furiously flung her things together. Her shoulders shook and Chase was sure she could see tears on Grace's hard face. The woman held her head high and her shoulders back as she marched out. Chase felt so sorry for her, she almost forgot that this was Grace Pilsen, a woman she couldn't stand.

At the end of the Batter Battle, when Anna was proclaimed the first-place winner, it was almost anticlimactic. The drama had been over when Grace left. Chase hoped that both Anna and Grace would compete next year to find out who was the true champion.

Anna felt the same way, she said, as they all walked together to the parking lot.

"I don't feel like I really won when my main competition wasn't there. I almost wish the whole thing would have been postponed for a week, until Grace was better. That would have been a real battle."

"You're too good for your own good," Bill said, squeezing her shoulders somehow, in spite of the fact that he was carrying three bags of her things.

Julie held the tray of the Blueberry Muffin Bars that the judges hadn't eaten. They had big plans for those, back at the Bar None kitchen.

On Sunday, at about ten in the evening, Eddie called Chase. She debated answering it long enough that her phone quit ringing. When it immediately started again, she picked up and told Eddie, "Hi."

"Hey, I got a great surprise for you. You gotta come by my store tomorrow morning."

"Eddie, it's my day off and I'm going to be terribly busy picking things up for the wedding." She wished! The bridesmaid dresses still weren't in.

"You won't be sorry. It won't take long, I promise. You'll love it. Come by around nine."

He hung up before she could protest further. It might be easier, she told herself, to go there. Maybe she could think of a way to tell him she couldn't see him anymore. She was so happy that Mike had shown up to help them celebrate on Saturday. When he'd walked into the Bar None through the rear door and gave her a peck on the lips, she knew that all the tension between them was gone and they were on solid footing now. She had laughed with Mike, and with Julie, Jay, Anna, and Bill, late into the night.

She'd been pleased when Mike told her that his cousin, Patrice, had decided to go to work for the police department, teaching them how to detect and foil pickpockets and thieves. They were paying her for giving the classes and even suggested that other police departments might want to hire her, if the initial session went well.

Before Mike left, he'd come upstairs to give her a proper good-night kiss after a few pets for Quincy, and she'd gone to bed in a haze of happiness and love. She was determined not to mess things up between them again.

On Monday, she drove to Eddie's Health Bar and arrived angry that she was there. Why hadn't she called Eddie back and told him she couldn't make it? She had a million things to do today.

His shop wasn't open yet, but he let her in as soon as he saw her at the door.

"Here's what I want to do for a wedding gift to Anna and Bill," he said.

With dismay, she saw he'd laid out a complete buffet on his sales counter. There were at least a dozen plates full of finger food.

"Go ahead, taste a few of my creations. I'm volunteering to cater the reception." He was grinning, waiting for her to tell him how wonderful he was.

"Eddie." She summoned up a reserve of patience. "The reception has been arranged for a long time. Someone else is doing it."

"The more, the merrier, right? Go on, taste something."

Everything on the counter was green or brown. There was no way.

"Eddie. I have to be honest. We can't use your food. And—"

"I'm not charging anything. You can just add this—"

"—and I can't see you anymore. I'm committed to Mike Ramos. I'm seeing him."

"Ramos? The vet?"

"Please don't call anymore. I can't see you. I've realized we don't have a thing in common. We need to quit seeing each other." She hurried out before he could say anything else. Starting up her car, she saw him coming out the door. She clicked her locks and sped away.

There. She had done it. Why had it taken her so long?

THIRTY-NINE

After lunch alone in her apartment—alone except for her furry guy, Quincy—Chase became aware of the sun streaming through her balcony French doors.

"You know what we should do, don't you?" She dangled the harness and leash and Quincy jumped up and came over.

"I think we've done it, old boy. I think we've conquered this leash thing."

As they strolled in the bright, crisp air, she called Anna.

"You were right."

"I usually am, but what about this time?"

"We finally have it mastered, the walking on a leash."

Quincy stopped walking to study a noisy junco in the tree above them. The small bird with its soft gray back and white breast sent out a trill that made Chase check her cell phone. Quincy swished his tail and walked on, his ears pointed rearward at the sassy bird.

"And Quincy likes it?" Anna said.

"He seems to. He comes running when I get the harness out."

"Be sure you fasten that thing, Charity. I don't want him finding a dead body two days before my wedding."

"I sure wish we could find the bridesmaid dresses."

"Oh, didn't Julie tell you?"

"I haven't talked to her."

"They came! Julie dropped them off on her lunch break a few minutes ago."

Chase had forgotten they were being sent to Julie's place instead of hers, since they received so many baking supplies already at her place.

Whew! "That sure is good news. Should I come over and try mine on?"

"Come over when Julie's off work and I'll see if they need altering."

What a relief. Chase couldn't think of a single other thing that needed doing before the wedding. The Bar None would close Wednesday and Thursday, Christmas Eve and Christmas, and Anna would be married Wednesday evening.

Feeling like she weighed less, Chase walked on, musing about life and death and murderers.

Was Ron North a thoroughly bad person or not? He had a borderline-dangerous habit of stalking women. Okay, it *was* dangerous, since it had driven Dillon Yardley to try to end her life to escape him. So she came down on the side of thoroughly bad for him.

Bart Fender must have been head over heels in love with Dillon, but that didn't excuse his actions. He must have been driven by knowing that his love wasn't enough to keep Dillon going. All of that was on top of his drug dealing. Bart's future would be decided by a jury, but Chase wondered what Dillon's would be.

On the other hand, Principal Snelson and Mr. Hail had been deliberately defrauding defenseless older people for their own financial gain. They were just as evil as the others involved in this whole mess. She chuckled to think of Mrs. Snelson throwing her husband's clothing in the dump. She had heard of women leaving their husband's belongings in the front yard, even in the rain, but never driving them to a dump.

It looked like Dickie Byrd's campaign had fallen through. The last time she drove past his headquarters, it was empty. A few of Monique's posters still clung to poles and stared out from shop windows, but most were gone. Monique had been seen in the company of a local bank executive. Dickie, Rich, or whatever he was called now, had left town. Chase was confident he would run for office somewhere else eventually. He'd been politicking his whole life.

They were now in front of the Meet N Eat, since it lay along their regular route. Another few pounds of weight lifted when she thought about how she was through fending off the charming, electric Eddie Heath. A person who ran a health food place had nothing in common with a person who baked decadent cookie bars.

Julie was tied up with the rest of the real estate case, as well as an additional one she had been given in an e-mail late Saturday. She had yet to celebrate not being a murder suspect, but Chase was making plans for that. They *would* celebrate. Exactly where and how and with whom wasn't clear, but Chase was thinking about it a lot. It would happen.

FORTY

"I'm sorry, Quincy," Chase said. "I promise we'll have a tree next year."

Quincy loved the small artificial tree Chase usually put up in her apartment. He didn't love the tree so much, though, as he liked batting the ornaments off and seeing where he could hide them.

This was the first year Chase hadn't had a Christmas tree. She hadn't had time, between going out to dinner with Mike twice, baking far into the night after that and every day since the Minny Batter Battle, and getting last-minute wedding tasks done in her spare moments. The reception seating was constantly being redone as regrets and acceptances came in. Some people "informed" Anna they would be bringing extra people. Had they never had to manage a wedding? It was almost impossible to fit in extra people unless enough guests canceled. Something had to give and it was her own tree.

Since the dresses had arrived two days before the wedding and Chase and Julie were at Anna's late the last two nights getting them fitted, there had been no chance for a bachelorette party. Julie promised they would have one after the wedding, somehow, somewhere.

Now, getting ready to walk down the aisle of the wedding chapel, she knew everything was worth it. Julie stood in front of her, her more petite figure showing off the asymmetrical one-shoulder design a bit better than Chase's did, or so Chase thought.

Chase peeked around Julie's shoulder to see the men lined up in front. Bill's son, Rick, stood beside his father. Next to Rick was an old friend of Bill's whom Chase and Julie had met half an hour before the wedding. Bill was appropriately pale and nervous in his handsome dark suit.

The padded pews held Anna's and Bill's dearest friends and a few distant relatives.

Anna stood behind them and around the corner, out of sight of her intended until the proper, dramatic moment.

The music changed to Edvard Grieg's ethereal "Morning Mood," the cue for Julie and Chase to start down the aisle. Chase waited for Julie to get four rows ahead, then she started the slow, unnatural, bridesmaid's gait: step, pause, step, pause.

Anna had tried to figure out a way for Quincy to act as

ring bearer, but Chase prevailed in talking her out of that. What chaos that would have been!

Mike looked up at Chase as she passed, melting her heart with his smile and those deep chocolate eyes. Mallory, close beside Tanner in the next row, sat with her left hand casually on top of her right, displaying the diamond promise ring he had given her two days ago at Bar None. Inger sat with them, smiling and happy, her baby bump getting larger every day.

Professor Andy Fear sat with his arm protectively around Hilda Bjorn. Hilda gave Julie a huge smile as she passed. The older woman never tired of telling Julie how grateful she was that Julie had saved her from selling her house and had put "that bad man" in jail.

That wasn't technically correct. Both Snelson and Hail were still awaiting trial and were free on bond, but they would eventually be there, Chase was sure. When the news reported that Principal Snelson's wife had hauled his clothing to the city dump on Sunday, the day after she had kicked him out, he became a topic of derisive conversation on the news media and in the Bar None shop. Footage of him fleeing reporters who were shoving microphones in his face replayed over and over on the nightly news. He had dropped out of sight, though. Maybe he was staying with Hail now, until their trials. If he hadn't turned out to be such a sleaze-ball, Chase could almost feel sorry for him.

When they reached the end of the aisle and turned to face the back of the chapel, Chase spied Grace Pilsen sitting alone in the last row. Her nose was still red and she wasn't completely healthy, but it was nice she had shown up. And very nice she was sitting far away from everyone else so she wouldn't infect them.

The music changed again. This time Mendelssohn's "Wedding March" rang out.

Anna, resplendent in the biggest smile Chase had ever seen and shimmering in a silk silvery, gray-on-gray dress, slowly walked down the aisle to become Mrs. William Shandy.

RECIPES

BLUEBERRY MUFFIN BARS

2½ cups unbleached flour
2 teaspoons baking powder
Pinch of salt
½ cup butter
1 cup sugar
2 eggs, beaten
½ teaspoon sherry flavoring
½ cup milk
1 cup fresh rinsed blueberries

Preheat oven to 375 degrees.
   Mix flour, baking powder, and salt in a small bowl.

In a large bowl, cream butter and sugar.

Add beaten eggs and sherry flavoring.

Add milk and flour mixture alternating, starting with milk, in three parts.

Rinse and pat dry blueberries. Fold into mixture.

Spread in greased 8½ x 11–inch pan.

Bake 15–20 minutes.

Cool completely before adding drizzle.

Drizzle Topping
   1½ cups powdered sugar
   2–3 tablespoons milk
   ¼ teaspoon vanilla

Mix thoroughly until thin enough to drizzle, adjusting milk.

LEASH-TRAINING TIPS
FOR CATS

First of all, you have to have a proper harness. Cats can't be walked with a collar and leash. As many cat owners know, collars don't stay on many cats. A harness especially made for a cat will contain her, though, if you fasten it. There is a strap that goes around Kitty's neck, and also one that goes under her tummy immediately behind her front legs. Most, if not all, are made of nylon and clean easily. If your cat just can't stand a harness, there is what's called a cat holster, made of cotton, and looks like a little jacket. They aren't as adjustable as a normal harness, so you'll need to do some measuring for that one.

You can use a regular leash or one that's like a bungee. They attach on the part of the harness that's on the cat's back, not on the neck.

After you've picked out the kind and color, take your time at first. Introduce him to the harness gradually, a little bit at a time. Let Tommy Cat sniff it and get acquainted for a few days before you try to put it on him. You can even hold it out to him with a treat in your other hand so he associates it with good things.

Just as with a horse, touch the harness to the cat in various places until Kitty doesn't flinch and accepts it. Then, you can put the harness on, but just for a few minutes. Different cats will get used to this at different rates. Associating treats here won't hurt, either.

As she gets used to wearing it, put it on her, still without the leash, and play with her while she has it on.*

Next step is to attach the leash and let Tommy Cat drag it around for a few days. Try to do this in a place where the leash won't hang him up on anything!

When you start to walk Kitty with you holding the leash, do it in the house at first and don't lead her. In fact, you may never be able to lead her all that much. You can lay down a trail of treats, trying for a straight line. After this is working well, you're ready to go outdoors!

For indoor cats, which is when you normally use a leash, be prepared for them to startle at everything until they get used to the great outdoors.

It's good to establish a regular time of day for walking, just as with dogs, so Tommy Cat will expect it then. However, cats don't do their business on walks like dogs do. Walking a cat is done to give them fresh air and something different to smell, see, hear, and experience.

Every step of the way, tell Kitty how well she's doing and don't spare the treats!

Another tip. It's a lot easier to train a very young kitten (in which case, you'll need different sizes as she grows). Quincy, of course, is a very smart cat and got trained quickly for his age. Be sure to do all the fasteners securely so your cat doesn't escape and find dead bodies.

Most of this information is from the ASPCA's site at aspca.org/pet-care/virtual-pet-behaviorist/cat-behavior/teaching-your-cat-walk-leash.

Extra tip from Bodge

Janet Cantrell is the national bestselling author of the Fat Cat Mysteries, including *Fat Cat at Large* and *Fat Cat Spreads Out*.

FROM *NEW YORK TIMES* BESTSELLING AUTHOR

JANET CANTRELL

THE FAT CAT MYSTERIES

Fat Cat at Large
Fat Cat Spreads Out
Fat Cat Takes the Cake

PRAISE FOR THE FAT CAT MYSTERIES

"Every ounce a delightful new cozy-mystery series."
—Paige Shelton, *New York Times* bestselling author

"A fun new series…Quincy is a delight."
—Kings River Life Magazine

"A delicious mix of desserts, stealthy stealing,
feline foraging and murder!"
—Fresh Fiction

"Charming…Cozy mystery readers will be purring with delight."
—MyShelf.com

facebook.com/TheCrimeSceneBooks
penguin.com